The Heiress and the Banker

Lynne Preston

BOSTOCK HOUSE PUBLISHING

ESTABLISHED 2025

ISBN: 978-1-0693280-5-2 (Hardcover)
ISBN: 978-1-0693280-4-5 (Paperback)
ISBN: 978-1-0693280-6-9 (Electronic Book)

First Published 2025

Bostock House Publishing

www.Bostock-House-Publishing.com

Dedication

I would like to dedicate this story, this fanciful tale, to my hometown in Mid-Cheshire. The Middlewich, although far away, which in spirit I have never left.

The Heiress and the Banker

Lynne Preston

Table of Contents

Table of Contents

Preface

The basis of this story first occurred to me one sunny Sunday afternoon during the Late-Seventies. At the time, along with myself, several members of my family were big fans of the romance novels. I started to talk about this story, the opening scenes etc., and my sister-in-law in particular kept asking, as she listened agog, "What happened next?"

Of course, this encouraged me to tell more of the story until she said, "Are you making this up as you are going along?"

Well, I had to admit that, at the time, I was. I do suppose though that anytime we write or tell a story of our own invention we are making it up as we are going along.

After that time I did not do any further development of the story of The Heiress and the Banker until the Mid-Nineties, at which time I was still using pen and ink. Shortly afterwards I acquired an IBM typewriter with replaceable typeball element. Of course, not too many years after that I was able to transfer this and other stories onto Word Documents using my first computer.

The main part of the story takes place during the spring, summer and autumn of 1975, the year I first left England for the big country. The 'Twenty or so years later', referred to in the epilogue, reflects the era in which I completed the original version of the tale.

The Heiress and the Banker
Prologue

Gillian strolled briskly along the winding drive that led to the manor house, the only home she had ever known. Her two dogs, Redfers and Blackie, ran on ahead. They looked around at intervals to yelp encouragement to their mistress.

"Oh, you pair!" Gillian said, laughing at the two red setters. "Can't wait to eat?" She broke into a trot. "Is that it?" she called out, her hiking boots scrunching in the gravel. "Famished again, as usual?"

Despite her cheerful demeanour, Gillian Brereton-Holbeck was not entirely happy with her lot. She had everything she could want, in the material sense, and never lacked love and affection from her parents, Lady Brereton and Colonel Holbeck. Yet, she felt that something was missing. In a few months time, Gillian would be twenty-one and the inheritance, Swiss bank account and all, left to her by her late maternal grandfather, would be all hers. She thought that maybe she could do something with that, after all, she did want an adventure. However, she did not really think that money was the answer. She had always had money. What Gillian wanted was to fall in love, be swept off her feet, like she imagined was the case for an ordinary girl.

"Twenty years old and never been kissed," she would often muse. Well, not kissed in the way she wanted to be kissed.

As they neared the manor house, the chauffer stepped out of the front door. He trotted down the steps to meet the dogs. Gillian saw him squat down and pull something from a pocket of his uniform coat.

"No, Frank!" she said, getting to the scene just in time. "No more biscuits, they're not good for them. They have their own doggie treats, no need for them to take yours."

The chauffer slipped the shortbread back into his pocket and stood up, patting the heads of both the dogs.

"Go on, then," he said to them. "Better listen to Miss Gillian." He smiled at her. "I'd best be getting on myself," he said. "The Colonel wants the Roller waxed and polished again."

"He'll have you polishing that car of his away, Frank," Gillian giggled. "Come on, you two." She set off at a trot. "Let's go see what we have for you to eat."

Gillian's home was situated in Occles-Leigh, a quiet village of thatched roofed cottages about four miles from the working class town of Middlewich. To the young men of that town, a young woman of Gillian's background was considered out of reach.

"And good for them!" the Colonel would often remark and, "Time you were looking to the future, my girl!"

Then he would humph and hah and pour himself a generous measure of brandy.

"Marry a man of good standing," he would advise, lifting the glass to peer at the amber liquid. "Someone of your own class." And, he would add, snifter poised ready, "I'm sure there are a lot of young hopefuls out there. Down the hatch, what?"

Gillian herself was certain there were quite a few 'Young hopefuls' amongst her circle of friends, but she did not so much as suspect that one of them, a very close friend, was most particularly hopeful.

The Heiress and the Banker
Chapter One
The Old Soldiers' Night Out

Gillian stood in the snug, drink in hand, nibbling hors d'oeuvres and chatting half-heartedly with a young fellow by the name of Cedric Ponsomby-Smythe. The occasion; the local old soldiers' reunion, retired officers only, please. The venue, as it seemed to be all too often to Gillian, was the 'Occles-Leigh Arms Hotel' on the Nantwich Road. A few minutes earlier, Gillian had agreed to go dancing the following Saturday night with Cedric. They would be going to the 'Cool Cat's Night Club' in nearby Nantwich. It had been an innocent sounding offer and Gillian didn't mind going to the dance in the least. She had known Cedric all her life, he being the son of Sir William Smythe, an old comrade in arms of her father's. The thought of him as a suitor had never entered her head.

The dashing Cedric, however, had different ideas. He thought, quite rightly, that Miss Gillian Brereton-Holbeck was a fine proposition. The encouragement of his father and the unspoken blessings of Gillian's, had been all he had needed to proceed. He did plan to introduce the subject of matrimony to his long time friend; but not tonight. Tonight was not the right time.

Cedric was presently rabbiting on about foxes and hounds; Gillian listening with half an ear.

"…then the Master of the Hunt came along to put a stop to it and…"

Gillian was not listening at all. Her attention was centred on the bar room.

She could catch glimpses of the activity in there by lowering her head slightly and peering through the serving hatch. The bar had, for a long time, held a certain fascination for her.

Ever since her father had forbade her to enter that den of iniquity, as he called it. Gillian had never yet been in there, but tonight… tonight!

Tonight the sounds drifting through the serving hatch intrigued her. The occasional voice raised in merriment; raucous laughter; snatches of music; the rattle of dominoes against a tabletop.

Our heroine made a decision. She was tired of always going along with her father's wishes; she was tired of the stuffed shirts in the snug. She was tired of Cedric's hunting stories.

"Excuse me, Cedric," she said. She deposited her empty glass on the tray of a passing waiter; he being a local lad making a few extra quid on a Saturday night. "I have to powder my nose."

"… thought they were out of sight, I suppose… What? Oh? I see. Right you are." He stepped aside to allow his friend.

Gillian, having thus made her excuses, gained temporary escape at least. She may have agreed to go dancing with Cedric, he had never yet stepped on her toes, but his stories she could do without.

Weaving her way around the other guests, she made her way to the door adjoining the lounge. The lounge, like the snug, was populated by retired officers and their guests. A smile here, a nod there, a brief hello, and she was at the door that opened onto the bar. She overrode the urge to take a deep breath (she didn't want a lungful of cigar smoke) and pushed the door open. Stepping resolutely over the threshold, Gillian entered another world.

A fire crackling merrily; an old dog lying on the hearth rug (its greying snout next to a saucepan of beer), the brasses on the mantelpiece above the fireplace. These were the features that first caught our heroine's eye.

The patrons, ranging in age from young to old, were engaged in conversation. Some attempting to be quiet and confidential, others loud and boisterous. Most, in company with others, were sitting at battle scarred tables. Others, like the fellows playing darts and the young blades gathered near the fire, were standing. The old hound appeared to tolerate this latter group with good grace, but he did seem to keep a close eye on the saucepan.

The dog lifted his head and, like the fellow standing, toe of one shoe on the white line, darts in hand, and the rest of the company, looked expectantly in Gillian's direction. Miss Brereton-Holbeck, for her part, suddenly realized that she must have been staring for some time and quickly set herself back into motion. She headed for the door marked 'Toilets'. It was in the far corner of the room.

The darts player, now mobile again himself, lofted a well-aimed dart into the bull's eye. He did a little jig, humouring no-one but himself, it seemed.

As she hurried across the black and white tiled floor, her formal evening gown gathering murmurs of appreciation, Gillian's eyes were drawn to a man standing alone at the bar. He looked to be of similar age to herself. As she stared, his sparkling blue eyes locked with her own. A smile lit up his face; she smiled in return… and she felt herself go giddy.

"Whew!" Gillian steadied herself with an effort, feeling those blue eyes on her the rest of the way across the room. It was with a great sigh of relief that she reached her destination.

Our heroine found that the door marked 'Toilets' opened onto a dimly lit passageway, the ladies' room being behind the first door on the left. Once inside the small room, she drew in a deep breath, then slowly exhaled with a sigh.

"What a hunk!" she said, looking herself over in the mirror above the sink. "What a hunk!" She patted her hair into place; checked over what little make-up she wore, then powdered her nose in actuality.

Once satisfied with her appearance, she returned her toiletries to her evening bag. She looked at herself again in the mirror, her mind running over the possibilities concerning her journey back through the bar.

The possibilities in connection with 'Blue Eyes', that is. Would he smile at her again? Would he be so bold as to approach her? Would he…?

"Won't find out standing here admiring yourself, Gillian," she told herself. With that, she turned away from the mirror, stepped back into the passageway and set off back the way she had come.

The sight of the blue-eyed stranger's leather-jacketed back, disappearing behind the rapidly closing door as he exited the premises, had not been a possibility Gillian had bargained for.

"That's that then!" she thought, with an effort at finality. "Back to the party."

≈ ≈ ≈ ≈ ≈

"Ahh! There you are, Gillian!" Cedric exclaimed on her return.

"Lucky sod!"

"Shush! Come join us, Gillian. Take no notice of him." He moved over to allow our heroine to join the group of which he was now a member.

"Cedric was just telling us…"

"I was just telling these chaps…" Cedric quickly interrupted, "and ladies…the one about the Scottish cloakroom attendant."

He looked around, defying anyone to gainsay him. "Have you heard that one, Gillian?"

"If you mean the one about Angus MeCoatup," our heroine said, with a sigh of resignation. "Many times, Cedric." Then, under her breath, "Almost as many times as the one about the Master of the Hunt and the courting couple."

"Oh dear! Ginny fizz, was it?"

"If I must," Gillian said then, relenting a little, "I'm sorry, Cedric. Yes, I'd love another ginny fiz."

Conversation amongst the group resumed as Cedric sought to catch the eye of a waiter. The topic of conversation just prior to Gillian's return from the powder room had not, of course, been about Angus MeCoatup. However, as stated earlier, Cedric would get around to discussing matrimony with the girl in question all in good time. Meanwhile, our heroine would not have to endure tales of the hunt alone.

After exchanging pleasantries for a while, Gillian slipped away from Cedric's group and circulated around the room. She greeted old friends, met new people, but her heart was just not in it. She was still thinking of the blue-eyed stranger and wondered whether she would ever see him again.

The Heiress and the Banker
Chapter Two
The Start of a New Day

Rodney Watkinson awoke to the realization that he was in unfamiliar surroundings. He lay still, peered around, only the top of his head and his eyes showing above the bedding. A small room with yellow curtains, the sun just coming up. The 'Occles-Leigh Arms', that was it. He had booked in here last night, his home away from home for he didn't know how long.

The 'Occles-Leigh Arms' in the village of Wimboldsley . He wondered where that was. He had seen the village sign by the roadside but, other than that, a couple of timber framed houses and this hotel, he had seen nothing but farmers' fields. He knew there must be a village somewhere; the people in the bar last night had surely not all driven up from Middlewich.

The people in the bar! The girl! Rodney's heart skipped a beat at the thought of her. He thought now that he should have waited for her to come out of the ladies' room, instead of calling it a night. He sighed, remembering how his breath had caught in his throat when she had returned his smile. But, what hope did he really have? She was a goddess; he was a bum in a leather jacket and jeans. Still, he did want to meet her and decided to ask Mrs. Braithewaite, the landlady, if she knew anything of her.

≈ ≈ ≈ ≈ ≈

That same Monday morning had found our Gillian, already dressed in her rough clothes, leaning out of her bedroom window. The sun was just beginning to appear over the horizon, its rays highlighting her shoulder length blonde hair.

She had volunteered to help out at the local Charity Shop in Middlewich this week and, between the anticipation of her new job and thoughts of 'Blue-Eyes', she had been unable to sleep past dawn. It was such a fresh morning and, as she breathed deeply of the fragrant air, she sighed, "Spring at last!" It had been a long winter and, although there was still a nip in the air, she decided to drive into town with the top down. Blow the cobwebs out.

Something flashing in the corner of her eye caused her to turn her head to the north, the direction in which her window faced. Another flash of light. Of course, that would be the weather-cock on the top of the Middlewich church tower. From its high vantage point, the weather-cock had silently marked countless dawns down the ages. This morning, has it had done since time out of mind, it was reflecting the rays of the steadily rising sun. The church tower itself would be visible soon, but Gillian wasn't going to wait for that. Not on this fine morning. There were dogs to walk and breakfast to attend to. With that in mind, she withdrew from the window opening and strode briskly from the room.

≈ ≈ ≈ ≈ ≈

Rodney looked at the dial of his alarm clock; ten-to-six. A bit early but our hero, not being one to lie musing in bed, threw the sheets aside. He swung his feet to the floor, yawned, stretched and sat on the edge of the bed to survey his surroundings in greater detail. A small room with heavy old fashioned furniture; a set of drawers, a wardrobe, a chair standing by the head of the bed and a rug covering the middle of the wooden floor. That and the bed was it. The yellow curtains, lit up by the early morning sun, provided the only bright spot in the otherwise cheerless room.

His gaze alighted on his suitcases. They were lying open, some of their contents spilling out onto the rug. He decided to deal with them after he had attended to his morning ablutions.

≈ ≈ ≈ ≈ ≈

When Gillian returned from walking her dogs, she fed and watered them, rubbed them between their ears and told them to be good boys. After that, she had showered and changed into fresh clothes.

Dressed casually in jeans, a yellow sweater over a blouse, white socks and sandals, she joined her parents for breakfast on the verandah.

"Good morning, mother! Good morning, father!" she said brightly, pulling her sunglasses down over her eyes.

"Good morning, Gillian," her parents responded in unison.

Her Ladyship and the Colonel, still in their housecoats, were seated at the table, breakfast already underway. Smithers, the butler, had just brought in a tray laden with the coffee things.

"Good morning, Miss Gillian," he said. He set the tray on the table and pulled out a chair for the young lady of the house.

"Good morning, Smithers!" Gillian settled herself into the seat, beaming a smile at the butler.

"What will be your pleasure, Miss?" he said, dolefully.

"A glass of orange juice and a bowl of cereal, please… It's such a lovely day… And a couple of slices of toast and marmalade would be nice, Smithers."

"Certainly, Miss!" The butler turned his haughty attention to Her Ladyship and the Colonel. "Will there be anything else, Madam? Sir?"

"Not for me, Smithers, thank you." Her Ladyship wiped the corner of her mouth with a napkin. "And we'll help ourselves to the coffee."

"As you say, Ma'am."

The Colonel lowered his newspaper. "You could ask Cookie to rustle up another kipper for me if you would, Smithers," he said, in his usual blustery fashion.

The butler bowed. "Very good, Sir!" With that, looking snootily down the length of his nose, he set off for the kitchen and the cook.

Gillian poured the coffee then, seeing as she was sitting with her back to the sun, pushed her sunglasses back to the top of her head. "It's such a lovely morning," she said. "I asked Frank to put the top down on my roadster."

"Dratted paper! Not worth reading these days." The Colonel tossed the newspaper aside. "What was that, my petal?" he said.

"I was just saying, daddy, it's such a lovely morning. I asked Frank to put the top down on my roadster."

The Colonel's monocle gleamed brightly in the sunshine.

"Off for a run, are you, my petal?"

"Gillian is working at the Charity Shop this week, Cuthbert. Remember?"

"Oh! Mmmph! That business? Well, I must say you sound awfully chipper about it."

Our heroine was in a chipper mood. She also looked positively radiant. However, his daughter having inherited her good looks from his side of the family, the Colonel saw no need to remark on this.

"It's a wonderful day, pappa, and listen to the chirruping of the birds. How could anyone be anything but chipper on a morning such as this?"

The Colonel agreed, albeit grumpily, then, "Blast these kidneys of mine! If you'll excuse me, my petals?" He rose from his chair, looked enquiring from wife to daughter. "Nature calleth."

"You really ought to see Doctor Drummond about that, Cuthbert. You were up three times last night."

"Making notes were you?" the Colonel muttered.

"What was that, dear?"

The Colonel hating, like most men, to bother with a doctor until he had to be carried to him on a stretcher (and not being so foolish as to repeat his earlier remark) said, "I was just saying, my petal, too much pugla-panni last night, what? A passing malady, no need to see the quack." He turned to go.

"I'll have Smithers make an appointment for you," Her Ladyship decreed.

The Colonel, muttering to himself about too much pugla-panni, went about his errand.

Once the ladies of the house were alone, Gillian, who had noticed her mother eyeing her curiously, enquired, "Yes, mother?"

"Gillian, you are looking positively radiant today, but that is hardly surprising, getting your good looks from the Brereton side of the family as you do. There is something in your eye though, and I dare say it has nothing to do with bird song or blue skies. Is it to do with young Ponsomby-Smythe? You two did seem to be getting on well last night. Your father will be pleased if…"

Gillian cut her mother off with a laugh. "Oh, mother! How could you think it? That twit Cedric indeed? I'd have to have four legs and a bushy tail for him to take any notice of me. Besides, he's like a cousin… we were just talking…"

"And?"

"Well, we are going dancing on Saturday night, but…"

"And?"

Our heroine was bursting to tell someone of the 'Blue-Eyed Stranger' and their brief silent communion in the bar the night before. She took a sip of her coffee, then told her mother all about her foray through that forbidden room.

"I'll see him again, mother, I know I will. When our eyes met, I felt something special."

"Well, I don't know what to say, Gillian. It's your life, but remember your father's warnings. Meanwhile, we won't mention any of this to him just yet… especially the bit about the bar."

"What's that about the bar?" the Colonel blustered, stepping back onto the verandah. He noticed the butler, hard on his heels.

"Ahh! Smithers! My kipper. Good man." He seated himself then, all mention of the bar forgotten, fell to with a will on his third kipper. The butler, meanwhile, served breakfast to the young lady of the house then withdrew haughtily into the background.

Gillian, after sharing a conspiratorial smile with her mother, got on with her breakfast. She had her sunglasses back in place; her eyes had given too much away already.

≈ ≈ ≈ ≈ ≈

Our hero, having returned clean-shaven and refreshed from his early morning duties, was busy unpacking.

He thought about the day ahead, his first day on a new job, that of assistant manager at the Middlewich Branch of Avonlea's Bank.

As he went about his business, he looked around the room again. It was his for two weeks, all expenses paid. After that, he was on his own. Well, he was a single man and, other than his old mother who now lived in Clapham Junction, he only had himself to worry about.

He had already done a reccy on the bank. After he had left the M6 at the Holmes Chapel exit, he had driven through Middlewich. It was on his way to the hotel anyway. He soon found Wheelock Street, the town being quite small. The bank itself was not exactly what he had been used to in London either. A sense of foreboding came upon him. Had he sentenced himself to the back of beyond? Still, Rodney Watkinson was an ambitious young man and, it not being what you know but who you know, and he not having connections in the right places, he had seen no alternative to advancement than 'The North'. Rodney felt sure that he would manage.

Once his suitcases were unpacked, he shoved them under the bed and dressed for the day ahead. His work clothes consisted of a dark pin-striped suit, white shirt, black tie, black shoes and grey socks. He would have preferred his jeans and leather jacket, which were where he had left them the night before. Thrown over the back of the bedside chair. However, in his business, certain standards had to be met.

Thus, with tie loosely draped about his open shirt neck, jacket over one shoulder and briefcase in hand, he made his way along the hallway to the back stairs and breakfast. His mouth started to water as he entered the small dining room.

"Mmm! Something smells good!" he said.

"Good morning, Mister Watkinson," the landlady called out.

Her be-scarfed and curlered head appeared around the door jamb from the kitchen.

"Would you like a cup o' tea while you wait, love?"

Rodney placed his briefcase on the carpeted floor. "Good morning, Mrs. Braithewaite," he said, pulling out a chair. "A nice cuppa would be just the job." He draped his jacket over the back of the chair and sat down at the table. This, he noticed, was the only place set. No other guests then; at least not for breakfast.

Our hero found himself facing a fireplace in the short wall opposite the door. This, cold and dark though it was, he thought, must be back to back with the one that had blazed so merrily in the bar the night before. The night before! Rodney's thoughts returned, unbidden, to the night before.

"Mrs. Braithewaite?"

"Yes, coming love." The landlady re-appeared carrying a tray, her wiry body wrapped in a well-worn pinafore. "Let me put this lot down," she said, unloading a teapot under a cosy, a large mug and the other accoutrements associated with a civilized breakfast.

"Mrs. Braithewaite," Rodney began again. "Last night, a young lady went through the bar. Blonde, beautiful, in an evening gown."

"Yes, well, 'appen as there was a lot o' young ladies like at the do last night. Now, if you don't mind, I 'ave to get back to me fryin' pan." The landlady knocked imaginary crumbs from the front of her pinafore. "Enjoy your cup o' tea, Mister Watkinson," she said, then scurried from the room.

"So!" Rodney thought, pouring himself a cuppa. "The old biddy knows who she is. Good!" That meant that 'Freya Vandanis Incarnate' was probably a local girl. Maybe the north wouldn't be so bad after all.

≈ ≈ ≈ ≈ ≈

Gillian emerged from the house wearing a windproof jacket. She had a bundle of old togs under each arm. These were a donation from her mother to the Charity Shop. The chauffer, having just brought Gillian's roadster round from the garage (top down as requested) stepped forward to help her.

"That's alright, Frank I can manage," Gillian said. She stepped lightly down the stone steps. "You can open the boot for me, if you would, please."

"Rutter, Miss Gillian," the chauffer said, stepping around to comply with her request. He looked at her sternly. "Rutter!"

Our heroine dropped the bundles into the open car boot and looked fondly at the chauffer. "Very well, Rutter if it makes you feel any better. I've had that lecture from the Colonel a thousand times."

"Miss Gillian," the chauffer replied. "For my own self, you can call me Frank whenever you've a mind to. It's your parents I'm thinking of, they don't like to be so familiar with the staff. I'd hate for you to get into any bother on my account." The car boot clunked shut.

"The staff I can understand, Frank, but to my mind that does not include you. I've known you all my life." She pinched the chauffer playfully on the cheek. "You're like one of the family and, what's more, I shall call you Frank and you will kindly cut out the Miss!"

Instead of answering, the chauffer stepped over to the driver's door of the Triumph and, opening it with a flourish, motioned for Gillian to enter.

Once she was behind the wheel, he closed the door. "Drive carefully, Miss," he said.

"I will, Frank. See you later." As she drove away, Gillian turned her head, blew the chauffer a kiss and waved.

Frank Rutter waved back and watched as the young lady of the house drove down the drive. She looked lovely, he thought, her hair tied loosely at the nape of her neck and fluttering in the breeze. He thought a lot of Gillian and sometimes liked to regard her as the daughter he had always wanted but now would never have. He had taught her a lot about the handling of the TR5, he being an enthusiast himself. He also maintained the car, of his own accord, to the same meticulous standards as he did the Colonel's Silver Cloud.

Frank had begun to wonder of late why Gillian did not have a steady boyfriend. Young Cedric was around the place a lot, but he did not count him. He had been around the place since they had been children. Still, he knew that Gillian did not lack for offers and, if he was thirty years younger, he would make her an offer himself. Oh well, he was too old and anyway, he was the wrong class of person to even have a look in there.

Our heroine now out of sight, the chauffer turned his attention back to that of polishing the Colonel's Roller.

Gillian had set off early in order to enjoy a drive through the lanes. She turned right at the bottom of the Manor Drive and pointed the nose of her roadster in the direction of Warmingham, a small village about four miles distant. This instead of turning left to the Nantwich Road and then straight on into Middlewich. As the car gathered speed, Gillian thought again what a lovely morning it was. The top down; wind in her hair; exhaust note reverberating in the narrow lanes. The TR's straight six engine purred smoothly as she cruised along. At this sedate speed, she could still hear the birds singing in the hedgerows.

There was no other traffic about as she passed the junction leading the back way into Cledford and Middlewich. There was a little copse of trees on this corner and Gillian wondered, not for the first time, what the purpose of the 'No Hunting' sign was. The sign had been nailed to one of the trees at some time in the past. What one could possibly hunt amongst those few trees she could not imagine.

Gillian's thoughts turned back to that of driving. Down into second gear, she turned right at the next junction, up to third, fourth, then back down to second for the ninety-degree bend.

Pulling out from the bend, she changed up to third. By the time she got back up to fourth gear, she had entered Warmingham. A long row of houses on the left, then down to third gear to descend the long hill into Warmingham proper. The village, as always, looked asleep. The 'Bear's Paw' at the bottom of the hill, with its bench seats in the little porch; the narrow humped back bridge over the River Wheelock; the village church on the opposite bank of the river. All was tranquil, basking in the early morning sun.

The church clock started to chime out the half-hour as Gillian pushed her foot down to climb the hill on the further side of the bridge. A gaggle of geese went flapping and hissing through a small farmyard, startled by the sudden thrapping of the TR's exhaust. Gillian laughed to herself.

"That woke someone up anyway!"

What a morning, the sky was so blue. "Like those blue eyes," our heroine mused. Where did he come from? Would she ever see him again? Who was he?

The blast of a car horn startled her out of her reverie. She pulled the Triumph sharply over to the left, narrowly avoiding a collision.

"Good job you don't have an extra coat of paint, old girl," Gillian muttered.

A few more miles and she was zipping through the hamlet of Copna-Grain; a row of houses and a working men's club.

"So much for that!" She picked up speed, the narrow Warmingham lanes behind her.

An easy cruise to Leighton, past the new hospital, then onto the Nantwich Road. Gillian had been looking forward to this, it was eight miles of foot to the floor, adrenalin pumping exhilaration.

The wide sweeping bends of this road called for a bit of speed. Our heroine, with throttle pedal hovering a hair's breadth from the backstop, gave the TR5 its head. She would barely back off the pedal until she was approaching the village of Wimboldsley. That village's older row houses and newly built estate lay south of the railway that formed the division between itself and the village of Occles-Leigh.

≈ ≈ ≈ ≈ ≈

Our hero emerged from the back door of his hotel, well fed and smartly turned out. He'd fastened his tie, done up his jacket and had neatly combed his jet black hair. Now, briefcase in hand, he found himself in a small cluttered yard. He made his way to the back gate. In the yard, Rodney noticed several beer barrels, a pile of old crates, an old mangle like his mum used to have (he still winced at the memory of trapping his fingers in that device all those years ago) and a dolly-tub and peg amongst the jumble of bric-a-brac.

The old dog from the night before was lying in his kennel, nose poking out through the door hole. The dog watched the interloper's progress disinterestedly. He made no attempt to get to his feet. He merely yawned and went back to sleep. Rodney, meanwhile, shut the gate behind him; perhaps not wanting the old dog to run amok in the farmers' fields.

Rodney looked around as he strolled to the car park. Fields, trees, more fields and cows eating grass. This was going to take some getting used to. Up until now Rodney had always been a city boy, he would miss the hurley-burley of that way of life. He'd miss his old mates as well and he wondered how his mum would manage. Well, he'd be back home at the weekend to tie up a few loose ends, and his mum was not without friends.

He rubbed his stomach. 'ilda, as Mrs. Braithewaite had instructed him to call her, had fed him royally. Bacon, eggs, black puddings, fried tomatoes, some of last night's mashed potatoes fried up, toast, marmalade and what felt like a few gallons of tea.

"You can call me 'ilda, young man," his landlady had said, whisking his clean plate from under his nose.

"Thank you, 'ilda," he had replied. "And you must call me Rodney." He had not mentioned his dream girl again, however. He had decided to leave that for another time.

Ah! There was his car, a dark blue Austin 1100, alone in the car park. He wondered briefly whether 'ilda had a car and, if so, where she kept it.

He tossed his briefcase onto the passenger seat, got behind the wheel and shoved the key into the ignition. The engine sputtered into life on the third try. He tapped the fuel gauge; the needle moved reluctantly, barely clearing the empty mark.

Rodney turned the radio on. 'The To-nee Black-burn Sh-o-w!' He gave the dial a twist. 'What's the recipe today, Jim?' Then shut the thing off.

He moved off, a stop at the car park exit to check for traffic.

"What the...?" His head spun like that of a spectator on the sidelines at Wimbledon as a bright red sportscar, blonde girl at the wheel, rocketed past. As he eased out onto the road, Rodney thought that if Jackie Stewart had a sister, then the girl in the red sportscar had to be her.

≈ ≈ ≈ ≈ ≈

Gillian had seen the blue Austin as she topped the rise over the railway bridge, just before the 'Occles-Leigh Arms Hotel'. Not wanting a road hog in front of her, she had slammed the throttle pedal fully home. The TR had leapt for the horizon and the newly budding greenery of the Cheshire countryside made a breathtaking rush towards her. The hotel and its car park were just a blur as she eased off and dropped down to third for the next bend.

A brief image had formed on our heroine's retina of a rubber-necked driver in the dark blue car. She eased her speed.

"I wonder...?" She glanced in the mirror. "Come on! Where are you?"

A quick glance over her shoulder. The road behind was empty.

"Achh! Probably not him anyway."

Gillian got on with the business at hand, she was now nearing Middlewich. Past the turn off into Occles-Leigh village, two or three children already at play in the school yard. The timber-framed houses on the left, the junction with the road from Winsford, and she was going down the hill to the outskirts of town.

The traffic lights at the aqueduct were green and she sped straight through.

Going up the hill on the other side of the tunnel, Gillian checked her rearview mirror. She noticed that, although there were no other vehicles on her side of the aqueduct, the traffic lights were already changing.

Around the new relief road, she turned by the church then drove on along Wheelock Street. A few of the townsfolks were already up and about as she turned in by the Charity Shop. She parked in a little space on the street known as Lawrence Gardens and shut the engine off. The six cylinder engine, already starting to cool, made ticking noises as she opened the boot and pulled out the bundle of old togs.

"Hello, Miss Gillian isn't it?"

Our heroine turned to look behind her. Two similar looking middle-aged ladies were approaching. These she recognised as the two sisters that ran the Charity Shop, Rebecca Smallwood and Rowena Price.

"That's right!" Gillian replied, beaming them a smile. "I spoke to you last week."

≈ ≈ ≈ ≈ ≈

Rodney began to mull that over in his mind. Jackie Stewart's sister? Or had it been she; the goddess from last night. Goddess or not, he knew he would never catch her in a month of Sundays.

Unbeknownst to himself, our hero was not far behind the girl of his dreams. He too noticed the children playing in the school yard; he saw the timber-framed houses of what he assumed to be the village of Wimboldsley and, once past the road coming up from Winsford, he descended the hill and saw the traffic lights at the aqueduct. There were just turning to red.

He stopped at the white line. No vehicles came through the aqueduct tunnel. He was still muttering to himself when he lights changed to amber.

"I wonder if they do anything exciting around here?" he thought. "Like watching the paint dry on the garden shed." He chuckled to himself. Yes, it would certainly be a big change from the city; 'The Smoke'.

Up the hill on the other side of the aqueduct, fine old houses set back from the road on either side, around the relief road and, turning by the church, Rodney entered Wheelock Street.

A few yards down the street and he swung his car into the public car park at the rear of the 'White Boar Hotel'.

Walking down the just awakening street, our hero heard the church clock striking the quarter-past-the-hour. Nicely done. He then noticed a portly figure, wearing a suit not unlike his own, approaching the same destination as himself. This had to be Mister Snoddlegrass, his new boss. Rodney quickened his pace in order to meet this distinguished looking gentleman at the front entrance to Avonlea's Bank.

≈ ≈ ≈ ≈ ≈

Gillian, relieved of her burdens, followed Rebecca and Rowena into the Charity Shop. Once inside, the two sisters walked over to a counter about twenty feet from and facing the front door. They set the bundles down and, with our heroine in tow, proceeded down a passage into a small back room. They removed their heavy coats and hung them on pegs by the doorway. Gillian followed suit, hanging her windbreaker on the one furthest from the door.

"Eeh! Let's 'ave a brew shall we?" the younger of the sisters exclaimed. She walked over to a counter and sink set against the back wall of the room.

"Well we usually do when we get here, our Rowena. I don't see as 'ow today should be an exception." Rebecca parked herself on a chair by the table in the middle of the room while her sister put the kettle on. "Eeh! That's better. Get the weight off me poor tired feet. It's me chilblains you know."

Rowena shoved an old toaster aside and set the kettle down on a hot plate. "We've only walked from home," she said. She turned to Gillian who had remained by the door. "To 'ear 'er talk you'd think as we'd just run a marathon. Th' ladies' toilets is just up the passageway if you want to freshen up, love," she said.

Gillian was feeling a little windblown, so she thanked her and went about that errand. When she returned, freshened up and hair brushed back into place, the two older ladies were sitting gossiping at the table. The tea was busily brewing in a pot set in the middle of the table. She pulled out a chair and sat down, wondering how anyone could stand to wear woolen skirts and thick cardigans on a warm morning like this.

"I was just sayin'," Rebecca said. "As 'ow that's a nice lookin' motorcar you 'ave there, Miss Gillian. An M.G. isn't it?"

"Just Gillian," our heroine replied. "And it's a Triumph actually."

"Oh yes?"

"Yes, a TR5. My parents gave it to me for my eighteenth birthday. It's a 1968. Five years old when I got it, but I really love that car. It's a bit faster than a TR6 and I think it is nicer looking as well."

"Very nice, I'm sure," Rebecca replied politely. "I've always liked M.G.s. Our Rowena's 'enry used to 'ave one at one time. Isn't that right, our Rowena?" Then, without waiting for an answer, "Well, I think as that tea must be brewed by now. I 'ope you don't mind powdered milk, Miss... Gillian, love. Milk won't keep in 'ere without a fridge you see."

"Powdered milk will be fine, thank you."

Gillian resolved that, around these two, she would keep her mouth shut about sports cars in general and her own in particular from now on.

≈ ≈ ≈ ≈ ≈

"Mister Snoddlegrass?"

"At your service," the older gent replied with a slight nod of his head.

"Good morning, Sir." Our hero extended his right hand. "I'm Rodney Watkinson, your new assistant manager."

The bank manager transferred his briefcase and newspaper to his left hand and took Rodney's in his right. "Samuel Snoddlegrass," he said. "Any trouble getting here?"

"None at all. Petrol shortage seems to be over, for now at least. The price has gone through the roof though."

"Aye, lad, scandalous. Over a pound a gallon they forecast before it's all over. I count myself lucky that I can walk to work. But not to worry, you're on expenses for a couple of weeks. Let Avonlea's pay, they can afford it. You'll not find me shy when it comes to signing chitties." He placed a companionable hand on Rodney's shoulder. "Let's get inside," he said. "We'll have a brew and a chin-wag before the rest of the staff arrive."

The two bankers looked a fine pair as they ascended the stone steps to the double front doors. The older man rotund and be-spectacled, a bowler hat jammed firmly onto his bald pate, briefcase and newspaper in one hand, keys of office dangling from the other; the younger tall and slim, crowned only by a full head of hair.

At the top of the steps, Mister Snoddlegrass unlocked and opened the doors (a task he had performed every day of his working life for the past thirty years) and ushered his new assistant manager into an enclosed vestibule. There was a glass paneled door to the left. The bank manager unlocked this door, opened it, nullified the alarm and, once more, ushered Rodney in before him.

Directly in front of the intrepid pair, once into the bank proper, were the counters behind which the tellers would sit. To their left, the front of the building, was a narrow wooden counter. Ball point pens on little gold chains stood at intervals along this well-polished customer convenience.

Rodney's eyes were now drawn upwards. High in the wall above the counter were two windows, through which the slanting rays of the early morning sun lit up a diffused patch on the wall behind the tellers' stations.

"This way, Rodney, lad." The bank manager had already set off towards the rear of the building.

"Sorry, yes."

"Would you like to come over for a spot of afternoon tea this Sunday?" Mr. Snoddlegrass said as Rodney approached. "I live just down Chester Road and I could make some introductions."

"Er… Well, I was meaning to talk to you about that Mister Snoddlegrass," Rodney said, striding in the manager's direction. "I have to return to London for the weekend and I was hoping to set off early on Thursday afternoon. Some loose ends to tie up, you know how it is."

"Highly irregular, lad, first week on the job and all, but I've no objections. None that matter, I dare say. You must come over another time then."

"The pleasure would be all mine, Mister Snoddlegrass."

"That's that settled then." Mister Snoddlegrass ushered his new assistant into his office. "Oh, and by the way, when it's just the two of us like this, call me Samuel. No need to stand on ceremony, lad."

"I'll try to remember that… Samuel and my apologies regarding the afternoon tea."

Samuel's office was behind a door set into the back wall of the rectangular main room. The door had a brass plate affixed to it bearing the legend, 'Manager'. Rodney had noticed in passing, a similar door, 'Assistant Manager', also embossed in brass, being the title of this office's occupant.

"Sit you down, lad," the bank manager said. He indicated one of the chairs facing the mahogany desk. "I'll make us a cuppa." He placed his briefcase and newspaper on the desk then set off to attend to the business of making a brew.

While Samuel hastened to an alcove off to the side of his office, Rodney picked up the newspaper.

'Petrol to Increase Another Ten Pence a Gallon'
'More Oil Shortages Expected'
'Petrol Rations Loom as Man in the Street Reels'
'Price of Natural Gas Soars to New Heights'
'Wage Freeze Delivers Knock-Out Blow'
'End of the World Predicted for Next Thursday Week'

Our hero scanned through the paper, finding more of the same. He threw it down in disgust.

"Aye, lad," Samuel said, stepping out of the small alcove. "I don't know why I bother with it myself. All doom and gloom these days. That's all you read about. Still, I suppose we shall muddle through somehow. North Sea oil'll tide us over for a bit." He hung his bowler hat on the hat stand then sat down at the desk.

"I understand that your mother brought you up alone, Rodney," he said.

"That's right. My dad never returned from Korea. He was with the British Commonwealth Forces over there. Lost his life at the Battle of Imjin River. I never knew him and mum never had the inclination to re-marry."

"Very sad, lad, very sad. We lost a lot of good lads there. Still, your mother did a good job of bringing you up, I dare say."

"Well, she did her best, Mister… Samuel and we never went short of anything."

"Aye, well, I've been a widower myself these past many years so I know some of what it must have been like."

The bank manager got to his feet. "How do you like your tea, lad?" he said, briskly. "It should be brewed by now."

"As long as it's hot and sweet it does me, Samuel. I'm not too fussy."

"Right you are, lad. A man of my own heart."

He hastened off to the small kitchen to return a few minutes later bearing two mugs of tea. "There y'are, lad," he said, placing the mugs on the desk. "Hot and sweet, just the way you like it."

By the time the brew and chin-wag were finished, Samuel Snoddlegrass had formed a very good opinion of his new assistant manager.

"I'm glad to see that you're ambitious, Rodney. You'll have your work cut out for you here. Mind you, at your age I was full of vim and vinegar myself. Aye, I've been at this game, man and boy, since 1927. I'll be retiring soon, as I'm sure you are aware?" Rodney nodded. "All being well, lad, you'll be moving into this office when I do."

"Well, that is my aim, Mister... Samuel, I don't mind admitting. I'd like to move up in the world."

"Aye, well, lad, handling people is not always as straightforward as it might seem. As I'm sure you've found out before now. Take our Miss Smith for instance."

"Oh?"

"You'll be meeting her shortly, lad. Don't worry about her. How do you find the 'Occles-Leigh Arms', by the way?"

"Comfortable enough. I did wonder at the high command's policy of billeting me out in the sticks with the 'White Boar' just down the street. Other than that, no complaints."

"Aye, well!" The bank manager began to fiddle with his empty tea mug. "That wasn't the high command, Rodney, lad, that was me. Brunhilde… Mrs. Braithewaite and I, go back a long way and well, since Mister Braithewaite passed away, I try to put business her way whenever I can. However, if you find it inconvenient?"

"Not inconvenient at all, Samuel, I just wondered why so far out of town. Now I understand."

Samuel raised a hand, palm outward, to forestall further comment. "Now then, lad! Brunhilde and I are just good friends. No more and no less."

"I never thought otherwise, Samuel," Rodney replied. "Never thought otherwise. She does make a good breakfast though, doesn't she?"

"She does that, lad, aye," Samuel replied. "She does that."

While the manager and his assistant had been thus engaged, the staff had been arriving. Mister Snoddlegrass, seeing a full compliment at last, invited Rodney to join him for introductions.

Samuel Snoddlegrass emerged from the office with our hero hard on his heels.

"Good morning, all," he said. Everyone looked his way. "We've a newcomer in camp today. My new assistant manager, Rodney Watkinson. Mister Watkinson, as by now you all know, joins us from a City branch. I've heard from on high as he is as keen as mustard and, I must say, I have to agree. That being so, I may just retire immediately." A pause for a diplomatic giggle or two. "Seriously though, I shall be slowly handing the reins over to Mister Watkinson and, all being well, this branch will have a new Old Man in a couple of months. Meanwhile, I'm sure that he can count on your usual helpful co-operation."

After this short speech, Rodney was introduced by turns to the staff: Mister John Yates (the middle-aged loans manager); Mrs. Marian Davies (the head teller); Mister Harold Hawthorne and Mister Arthur Woodbine (both tellers and of similar age to Rodney)… and then there was Roxanne Smith.

Miss Smith was quite young, around twenty our hero guessed. Five foot two inches tall and very well proportioned. She had shoulder length black hair, hips that had a way of swaying provocatively without even moving and a smile that said, "Hello, Mister Watkinson. Pleased to make your acquaintance," in as sultry a tone as Rodney had ever heard.

Mister Snoddlegrass stepped forward. "Miss Smith, Mister Watkinson?"

"Oh, sorry, Miss Smith. I was miles away. The pleasure is all mine, I'm sure."

He took hold of Miss Smith's hand, giving it a gentle squeeze. Roxanne smiled, tickled his palm with her middle finger and winked. Rodney's eyes popped a little and, on letting go of the young trainee's hand, unconsciously loosened his tie. The rest of the staff had already drifted back to their work stations and Mister Snoddlegrass, anxious perhaps to get back to his teapot, said, "I'll be in my office if you need anything, Mister Watkinson, Miss Smith will help you to settle into yours." He then added, with a secret chuckle, "Our Miss Smith will be acting as your personal assistant, by the way."

"Thank you, Mister Snoddlegrass," Rodney said, to the retreating bank manager's back. He then returned his attention to Miss Smith. He was certainly going to have to speak to her about the dress code. A mid-thigh length black leather skirt was not quite what Avonlea's expected, his own personal opinion aside. As for those Gypsy Lil earrings? He would have to see. However, there would be time for all that, in the meantime there was the matter of his office.

"Well, Miss Smith," he began. The rest of his words were cut off by a rattling at the door. Like everyone else in the bank, he looked in that direction.

Rodney's jaw dropped and he stared in disbelief. It was she… the girl of his dreams… she was dressed like an ordinary mortal and waving something at him. Our hero could see that the goddess's mouth was moving and realized that he had to get his shut and the door open… before she de-materialized or something.

The Heiress and the Banker
Chapter Three
They Meet

Our heroine and the Charity Shop ladies, like our hero and his new boss, had had a good gossip that morning. However, they had soon got busy once the tea was finished. The three of them had set to work attaching price tags to the old togs donated by Gillian's mother. Once priced, the articles were hung on the racks that cluttered up the front space of the shop. Pride of place went to a Saville Row suit. This garment was hardly worn, however, it was no longer a match for the Colonel's ample girth. At five pounds, it was the most expensive item on display.

The task of pricing and hanging complete, Gillian pulled out a twenty pound note from her pocket and offered it to Rebecca as a float for the till.

Rebecca had been taken aback. It was, after all, the highest currency note in circulation at the time. "That's very generous, Gillian," she said. "Too generous, but if you insist it would 'ave to be in smaller denominations than that to be of any use."

"That's alright," our heroine replied. "I'll nip down to the bank and get some small change. Won't be a minute." And off she went, stepping breezily along Wheelock Street, to Avonlea's Bank.

What? The door still locked? "H-e-l-l-o-o! Are you open?" Gillian had the attention of a dark haired girl who had been gazing earnestly into the eyes of a young man. "Y-o-o-H-o-o!"

The young man turned around. Our heroine was dumbstruck. It was he; 'Blue-Eyes'. Yes! It had to be him. He looked a little different wearing a suit, his mouth hanging open and his eyes popping out, but it was definitely him.

"H-e-l-l-o-o-o!"

At last he was coming over to her... half a stride behind that Jezebel.

Miss Smith beat Mister Watkinson to the door by a scant half-step. She yanked it open, causing Gillian to tumble through the opening. She almost fell into Rodney's arms, but caught herself just in time. Our hero stumbled backwards, caught himself then, with an embarrassed grin, faced his dream girl.

His entire field of vision was taken up by the most enchanting young woman he had ever seen in his life as he stammered out, "Good morning, Miss... er... Miss... er... Can I help you, Madam?"

"Well, you could call me Miss Brereton-Holbeck. Gillian, if you prefer."

"Of course, Gillian." His eyes never left hers. "And how may I help you?"

"Well, I need some small change for this," Gillian said. She brought the twenty pound note into view. "Mister erm...?"

"Oh, yes, sorry." Rodney reached into his inside pocket, pulled his wallet out. "Rodney Watkinson. I'm the new assistant manager here." Reluctantly, our hero pulled his eyes away from hers, just long enough to scrutinize the contents of his wallet. He pulled out a tenner and two fives, all the cash he had on him. He offered the notes, fumbled the twenty but did manage to get it into his wallet.

"Miss Brereton-Holbeck... Gillian..." Shivers ran down our heroine's spine at the way her name fell from his lips. "Do you have a sports car? A red one? A TR4 perhaps?"

"I have a red TR5 actually."

"Then it was you...?"

"This morning?" she finished off, with a laugh.

"That's right. A TR5 did you say?"

"Yes!" Gillian pocketed the 'loose change' from Rodney's wallet and turned to go. "I have it parked in Lawrence Gardens if you would like to take a closer look?" she said, then, over her shoulder, "Lunch time, perhaps? I'll be in the Charity Shop."

"I'll be there," Rodney replied. "Promise."

"Good! I'll see you then." With that, Gillian breezed out the door, Rodney's eyes following her every inch of the way.

≈ ≈ ≈ ≈ ≈

Roxanne Smith had never seen such a performance in her entire young life. She had looked, open-mouthed herself, at first one then the other.

"'I have a wed TR5 actuawwy'," she mimicked. "'Lunch time, perwaps?' The hussy! Starting tomorrow this skirt is two inches shorter. Finally get a bit of class around here and 'Y-o-o-H-o-o! Could I have some small change for this, Mister?' I'll wear my garter belt to work as well. The hussy!"

Rodney, almost back to Earth, had been observing Miss Smith's antics. "Yes, Miss Smith?"

"Oh! I er... I'll show you to your office now, Mister Watkinson," she said. "If you will walk this way?" And off she slinked, Rodney once again half a stride behind her.

≈ ≈ ≈ ≈ ≈

Miss Smith had not been the only witness to the little melodrama by the front door. The rest of the staff had also been enthralled by the scene, Mister Snoddlegrass included. He had left his office door ajar.

"Well, well, well," he had thought to himself. "Our Mister Watkinson certainly likes to aim high. Miss Gillian Brereton-Holbeck no less."

However, Miss Brereton-Holbeck had seemed most encouraging and Rodney's personal life was no concern of his. Young Roxanne? Now she was a different kettle of fish altogether.

Things could get very interesting around Avonlea's Bank Middlewich in very short order.

Samuel sat back and took a mouthful of tea from his replenished mug. Hot and sweet, the way he liked it.

"Roxanne Smith could certainly be that when she chose to be," he thought. "Hot and sweet." He sat forward abruptly, overtaken by a coughing fit.

"Are you alright, Mister Snoddlegrass?"

"Just some tea gone down the wrong way, Mrs. Davies," he wheezed. "I'll be alright."

"Silly old duffer," she muttered.

Mrs. Davis thought about the situation she could see developing. Miss Smith, Mister Watkinson and Miss Brereton-Holbeck; it could quickly become out of hand.

≈ ≈ ≈ ≈ ≈

Gillian could have hugged everyone she met as she strode briskly along back to the Charity Shop. What a wonderful world! What happy co-incidence! Her 'Blue-Eyes' her 'Dream Boat', the new assistant manager at the bank. Gillian could tell he was from London, his accent stood out a mile.

"Good morning, Elisha!" she called out, addressing a young woman on the other side of the street.

Elisha, like Gillian, was a member of S.P.A.C.E., the society that ran the Alhambra cinema. She was in the process of pasting posters to the picture house's ornate false front.

"Good morning, Gillian," she called back. "We've got a new film this week, 'The Man with the Golden Gun'. James Bond."

"Great! I want to see that myself," Gillian said happily then, to herself, "With Rodney Dream-Boat, of course."

Elisha waved and returned to her work as our heroine proceeded up the street.

The aromas from 'Rhodas' Pâtisserie' made her mouth water as she passed the gentlemen's outfitters on her side of the street. Well, maybe Rodney Blue-Eyes would like to go for lunch at Rhodas', it was something to look forward to.

Gillian felt that she was walking on air. "Good morning, Mister Costello!" she said. "Nice day for selling vegetables."

"It is that, lass, aye! It is that." The greengrocer stopped in his work to admire her sprightly gait as she progressed along the street.

Everyone she met along Wheelock Street found themselves infected by her good humoured charm. When she got back to the Charity Shop, she opened the door and stepped inside with a flourish.

"Your small change, Rebecca," she said, handing over the tenner and two fives. "I'll wash the front windows for you if you like. I'm bursting with energy."

"More power to you, girl," Rebecca said, putting the banknotes into the till. "You'll find a bucket and wash leather under th' sink, th' step ladder's in th' back yard."

"You can do my windows next if you like, love," Rowena said. "Up Darlington Street. It's just over the way."

"I might take you up on that," Gillian said happily. She set off for the back room. "How about your place, Rowena?"

≈ ≈ ≈ ≈ ≈

Rodney spent most of the morning organizing his office and getting to know the staff a little better. Apart from a tea break together at half-past-ten, he had not seen his boss.

Shortly before noon, he was ensconced behind his desk, apparently studying a ledger. A tap on the door was quickly followed by Miss Smith entering his office. She was briefly silhouetted in the doorway by the bright noonday sun.

Swinging the door shut with her foot, she sashayed over to the desk; a folder clutched tightly to her chest.

"Thank you, Miss Smith," Rodney said without looking up. "I'll see to that lot later on."

Roxanne leaned over the desk and placed the folder down, right on top of the ledger. Rodney looked up with some annoyance.

"Miss Smith…?" he said, with a sharp intake of breath.

"Will that be all, Mister Watkinson?" Roxanne breathed. The top four buttons of her blouse were undone. "Or will there be anything else?"

With an effort, Rodney raised his eyes to meet those of his assistant. Miss Smith stood up to fill her lungs, at the same time buttoning up her blouse. She gave Rodney an inviting smile.

"I think that that will be all for now, Miss Smith," Rodney said, hoping that his cheeks weren't as red as they felt. "You may as well go for lunch if you like," and, under his breath. "Take a cold shower while you're at it."

"Thank you, Mister Watkinson," Roxanne breathed. "And don't forget your date."

Rodney opened his mouth to answer, but Miss Smith had already turned sinuously on her heel and, gracefully as a cat, was leaving the office.

"That girl is definitely in the wrong line of work," he muttered.

≈ ≈ ≈ ≈ ≈

Roxanne had no sooner cleared the front steps of the bank than Rodney was stepping out of his office. Descending the steps from the bank, he removed his tie and opened his shirt collar. He stuffed his tie into a pocket, then lengthened his stride purposefully in the direction of Lawrence Gardens.

The church clock began to hammer out the twelve strokes of mid-day. Roxanne was visible on the other side of the street, hem of her skirt doing a little dance as she quick-stepped around slower pedestrians. She was going in the same direction as Rodney and it was with some relief that he saw her step into 'Rhodas' Pâtisserie'.

"At least she isn't going window shopping at the Charity Shop," he thought. Something he would not have put beyond Miss Smith's imagination.

$$\approx \approx \approx \approx \approx$$

Our heroine, who had kept an eye on the street through the now gleaming front window, came out of the shop to meet her Dream Boat.

"Hello again!"

"Hello," Rodney replied, trying not to get lost in the blue of her eyes. "How was your morning?"

"Busy, but never-ending."

"Ditto!" our hero replied, his eyes never leaving Gillian's.

"Come on, I'll show you the motor." Gillian led the way around into Lawrence Gardens. "It's around here."

"Nice! Very nice, Gillian," Rodney said, walking around the TR5. "I'm surprised you left the top down though."

Our heroine felt a pleasant sensation run through her body at the way he sounded her name. "Oh, they are decent folk around here," she said. "And I come out now and again to check up."

"It still looks like a TR4 to me," Rodney said.

"Not surprisingly. The body is the same as a TR4A," Gillian explained. She lifted the bonnet. "But the engine, therein lies the difference."

Rodney looked admiringly into the gleaming engine bay. "A straight six?"

"Two and a half litres worth," Gillian said. "Fuel injected to boot."

"Impressive! Although cars aren't my strong point."

"Oh, that's alright. This is a 1968. In 1969, they brought out a redesigned body."

"The TR6?"

"Exactly! But the TR5 is still better looking." She closed the bonnet with a thunk.

"Nice car, Gillian…" Rodney paused as he watched her tilt her head beguilingly. "…erm… Must be getting expensive to run?" he went on, with some effort. "Especially these days."

"It's not too bad. TRemor returns around twenty miles to the gallon and I don't count every penny. It's my hobby you see."

"Yes, when it's your hobby you don't count the cost so much," Rodney replied doubtfully. "You call the car Tremor?"

"Tree-more," she pronounced. "Tree-more, TR-E-more, TRemor. TR5… Tremor. Get it?"

"Yes, I see. Faster than a TR6 did you say?"

"A little… and I know," she replied with a mischievous grin. "I'll take you for a spin sometime if you like?"

"Well, we've only just met but, yes, count me in. Will I need a parachute?"

"No! It would be useless. I like to fly low. It would never open in time." Gillian smiled. "Have you had lunch, Rodney?"

"My turn to say no. Do you have a suggestion?"

"If you fancy a pastie, 'Rhodas' is just up the street."

A picture of Roxanne Smith entering that same establishment ran through our hero's mind.

"My treat?" Gillian said. She walked around the car, took hold of his hand. "Come on!" she said and set off in the direction of the patisserie. Thus they walked, side by side, up the street.

"Well, Gillian," Rodney said. "My first day up north and already I've been taken in tow by a girl. A very charming girl at that."

"Why, thank you, kind sir," Gillian replied.

Our hero, being one for striking while the iron is hot, said, "I noticed that there's a James Bond playing at the pictures this week. Do you fancy going? Tonight? With me? My treat this time?"

"I'd love to," Gillian said. "I'll meet you in 'La Trev's Wine Bar' at eight."

"'La Trev's Wine Bar'?"

"It's what we call it. Opposite the 'White Boar'. But first, lunch."

With that, and hand in hand, the happy pair entered 'Rhodas'.

A long glass-panelled counter on the left with several customers queued up; a tiled floor; a large plate-glass front window (in need of spring cleaning); half-a-dozen round topped tables along the wall on the right... and mouth-watering aromas. That was 'Rhodas'.

Roxanne Smith was seated at a table in the far corner of the room. She was busy licking the cream out of the centre of a chocolate éclair. Her actions bordered on the improper, while her sweet young face retained a completely innocent expression. Rodney caught a brief glimpse of thigh as she crossed her legs under the table. She winked at him as her cream covered tongue slipped evocatively between her lips and back into her mouth.

Rodney's eyes popped, as at his first meeting with young Miss Smith.

Gillian, still hand in hand with our hero and standing at the counter with him, asked, "What does Jezebel do at the bank?"

"'Jezebel'?"

"Over there in the corner." Gillian indicated Roxanne with a flick of her head. "The tart with the tart."

"Oh... That's our Miss Smith. She's a trainee. Does a bit of everything."

"Mmmm! I'll bet she does."

"Can I 'elp you, ducks?"

Rodney turned to find himself confronted by a white smocked lady. She looked at him across the counter, eyebrows furrowed.

"Two Cornish pasties and a pot of tea, please," Gillian said, drawing the lady's attention her way. "And... Chocolate éclair, Rodney?"

"Oh... er... Not for me, thanks," he said hurriedly, trying not to glance, but doing so anyway, in Roxanne's direction.

"Two pasties and a pot o' tea then, ducks?"

"Yes, please," Gillian said.

"Rhoda will bring it to you when it's ready. You two go and sit yourselves down."

"See you back at the office, Mister Watkinson," Roxanne trilled sweetly, her oral adventures with the éclair now being over.

"Yes, see you later, Miss Smith," Rodney said in a neutral tone as he watched her trip lightly out the door.

"Shall we?"

"... er... Yes, of course." Rodney led the way to one of the tables over by the wall. "This suit you?"

"Yes," Gillian replied, thinking how she would like to turn 'Miss Smith' loose under Cedric's nose. She thought that it would be fun watching him trying to run that fox to earth.

"You're from London, then?" she asked once seated.

"Is it that obvious? Clapham Junction actually and no, I'm not a Cockney. You have to be born within the sound of Bow Bells."

"If you say so. I love your accent, whatever it is."

The colour rose in Rodney's cheeks. "And what about you?" he said. "Where did you take off from this morning? You were flying awfully close to the ground when I saw you."

"Yes, I did warn you." Gillian laughed. "I'd been for a potter through the lanes then decided to blow the cobwebs out along Nantwich Road."

"You live in Middlewich?"

"Occles-Leigh. A small village not far from here. You may have noticed the school on the corner."

Before Rodney could reply, a shadow fell across the table.

He looked up to see a large red-faced lady holding a tray. She was attired in a similar get-up to the lady that had taken their order. She deposited the tray firmly on the table.

"Enjoy yer dinners," she said. After placing the bill face up on the table, she stood back, looking from one to the other.

Gillian paid up and, after the big lady had crashed back through the swing doors into the kitchen, Rodney, awe struck, asked, "Is that Rhoda?"

"There are two Rhodas, Rodney." Gillian picked up the plate and pastie closest to her then went on. "That particular Rhoda is 'Little Rhoda'."

"What?" Rodney gasped.

"No need to look so stricken. I'm joking. Little Rhoda took our order."

With a sigh of relief Rodney picked up the teapot. "Shall I be mother?"

The Heiress and the Banker
Chapter Four
Monday Night at the Movies

Gillian took her time preparing for her date that evening. After bathing, she put on her favourite bathrobe then sat at her dressing table to blow dry and brush her hair. Once satisfied with this, she unplugged the blow-dryer and placed it and the brush on the dresser's oaken top. Rising from the stool she removed her bathrobe, threw it onto the bed then put on fresh underwear.

Sitting once more on the stool and stretching out one leg at a time, she rolled on black pantyhose. While still seated, she put on a white silk blouse.

Gillian had decided to wear a mid-thigh length skirt, also black, for the evening and now stepped into this, tilting her pelvis slightly as she pulled it into place. Fastening the rear attached zipper and then the waistband, she admired herself in the mirror.

Placing one hand on her flat midriff, she thought, "Not bad really, considering I'm pushing twenty-one." She then selected a black lightweight cashmere sweater and, gathering it into her hands, pulled it over her head. Arms into the gentle caress of the sleeves and snug fitting body pulled down over hers, she was almost ready.

Sitting on the stool once more, she fastened a lightweight gold chain around her neck. Pulling down one earlobe at a time, she inserted a pair of gold studs, then slipped her favourite bracelet onto her wrist. Now, a little perfume, a touch of make-up, another quick brush of her hair and, stepping into her shoes, she stood up.

≈ ≈ ≈ ≈ ≈

Meanwhile, down Middlewich, Rodney strolled into 'La Trev's Wine Bar', leather jacket open and hands stuffed into his jeans' pockets. He was fifteen minutes early. He had his white roller-necked sweater on tonight and wished he could have ridden his motorbike up from London. He was sure that Gillian would enjoy riding pillion with him. The bike, an old Triumph Thunderbird, was not the fastest thing on two wheels, but it was fast enough. He had not mentioned it yet, preferring to let Gillian demonstrate the prowess of her TR5 first. Once he had a more permanent place to stay, he would bring his bike up north, then it would be his turn in the sun.

"Good evening, Sir!"

Rodney turned his attention to his host.

"What will be the young gentleman's pleasure tonight? Table for one?" he said, approaching his first customer of the evening.

The host wore a beret, horizontally striped jersey, black pants and black and white shoes, giving him the appearance of a French mime.

"Just a coffee, please," Rodney replied. He continued on to the bar and parked himself on one of the stools.

"Certainly, Sir! I'll just be a few moments."

Rodney thought his host to be a strange character to say the least. He looked to be about the same age as himself.

"Calling me a 'Young gentleman'?" he muttered.

He took in his surroundings; tables with plush red coverings, a red unlit candle in wax laden holder forming the centrepiece of each one. Heavy drapes, matching the colour of the tablecloths, framed the front windows. Posters of French provincial street scenes hung at intervals around the walls.

"That explains 'Monsieur's outfit anyway," Rodney thought, 'Monsieur' having disappeared rather abruptly into what was presumably the kitchen. "And why they call him 'La Trev'."

He glanced through a menu he found at his elbow and pictured 'Big Rhoda' waiting on in these surroundings. He thought that the proverbial 'Bull in a China Shop' would take a poor second place.

"Mmm! Expensive… and chips with everything."

He returned the menu to the bar top just as his host reappeared.

"Your coffee, Sir."

"Thank you! My name's Rodney, by the way." He offered his hand across the bar.

"Trevor." They shook hands. "Pleased to meet you. That will be thirty pence, please."

A little steep, but Rodney handed over the correct amount of change without comment.

"Just passing through," Trevor asked, turning back from the till.

"Actually, I'm with Avonlea's Bank. The new assistant manager."

"Oh, very good, Sir. We'll probably be seeing more of each other. You should have said. I'm the proprietor here. Maitre de and chief bottle washer. My sister, Mavis, is the cook. We do our best. Not much business on a Monday night. Too much on the telly, I suppose. You're from London?"

"Clapham Junction. Found out today that I have an accent. I always thought as it was you lot as had the speech impediment."

"That's a good one, coming from a Cockney Sparra!"

"Oh, I'm not a Cockney. Close as makes no difference up here I suppose."

"Yes, quite so," Trevor said. Then, stepping from behind the bar. "Well, must get on."

Our hero was left in peace to enjoy his coffee until Trevor returned to his station behind the bar.

"How's the coffee, Sir?"

"Nice enough." He pushed the empty cup in Trevor's direction and glanced at his watch. It was already past eight.

"Refill, Sir? Or do you have to be somewhere else?"

"Mmm?"

"Another cup, Sir. Would you like one?"

"Well… I do have a date… she should be here any minute." He glanced at his watch again. "We're going to see James Bond."

"Quick workers you Londoners. Not learned the language yet, and already stealing our women off us." Trevor picked up the empty cup. "Re-fill's on the house." He topped the cup up and pushed it over to Rodney. "This time. I preferred Sean Connery myself," he added.

"But then Roger Moore has a style of his own," Rodney said absently, glancing once again at his watch.

"Bit of history behind the Alhambra you know?"

Rodney stirred his coffee.

"Almost closed the place down once, they did." Trevor wiped the counter top with a damp cloth. "About ten years ago it was, but Colonel Holbeck saved it. Formed a society to keep it open, funded it with his own money. Couldn't bear the thought of it becoming 'Yet another bowling alley' or, even worse to his mind, 'A ballee snooker club'."

"He doesn't like snooker then?"

"Loves it, that and billiards. Always playing with his balls from what I hear." Trevor slapped at his thigh, laughing at his own joke. "Just didn't want to see the Alhambra turned into a club."

Our hero chuckled politely. "Colonel Holbeck, did you say?"

"That's right," Trevor said, wiping tears from his eyes.

"Would that be Brereton-Holbeck?"

"Lady Brereton is his wife. You've heard of him then? Good looking daughter as well. Comes in here sometimes with her friend Aysher. I wouldn't say no, I can tell you."

"So she's the colonel's daughter," Rodney muttered.

Trevor came from behind the bar again and went over to one of the front windows.

"O' course," he said, pulling the drapes closed. "Blokes like us stand no chance there… Unless she was out for a bit o' rough, that is." He went over to the other window, and his chin almost bounced off the floor. The Brereton-Holbeck's Roller was pulling up at the kerb, Gillian herself reclining in the back seat.

"Are you expecting Miss Gillian, Sir?" he said, the colour rising in his cheeks. He had been trying to curry favour at the bank… and now.

"I am, but don't worry about it." Rodney's face broke into a grin as he strode over to the door. "She probably just fancies a bit o' rough."

"Catching flies, Trevoire?" Gillian said as she breezed in.

Trevor mumbled something unintelligible. The Rolls Royce pulled smoothly away as he closed the second set of drapes.

"Hi, Blue-Eyes! Sorry to have kept you waiting."

"It was worth it, Gillian. You look terrific."

"Thank you. You're not so bad yourself."

"What?" Rodney pulled at his leather jacket. "This old thing?" He took Gillian by the hand. "Did you trade TRemor in or something?"

"Oh, the Roller? That's daddy's motor. Thought you might like to give a girl a ride home."

"I wouldn't want it any other way," Rodney said. "Shall we away to the pictures? You can tell me all about daddy's motor on the way. Not that it really interests me with you around."

Our heroine was certainly feeling swept off her feet as she walked, hand in hand, with her 'Blue-Eyes' the short distance along Wheelock Street to the Alhambra.

The audience from the earlier showing was coming out as our happy pair arrived. A dozen or so others were waiting to go in.

"A bit sparse for James Bond isn't it?" Rodney said. "Down the Smoke there' be…"

"You're not down the Smoke now, Rodney. This isn't London, so get used to it."

A few minutes later, they were at the ticket booth. "Two for the Circle, please, Aysher."

Aysher's eyes flicked from Gillian to Rodney and back.

"He's paying."

Rodney dutifully paid for the tickets, surprised that he had not been introduced.

"Little tease," Aysher muttered as the pair started out for the staircase.

"Scared she'll steal me off you?" Rodney said.

"Oh, there's no chance of that. I can be a jealous cat and she knows it. Do her good to be kept guessing. Hello, Percy."

"Evenin', Miss Gillian," Percy said, standing at ease by the Circle door. "Who's your friend?"

"Rodney Watkinson," our hero said, extending his right hand.

"Percy Smithwick." After a brief handshake, Percy, flashlight in hand, led the way to the Circle seats. Our happy pair, quite naturally, settled for two seats in the back row.

"Thanks, Percy," Gillian said as they settled into their seats.

"Any time, Miss Gillian, lass, any time." Percy turned to go. "Keep your eye on her, lad," he said. With that, he worked his way back to the door.

"He seems a decent chap," Rodney said.

"Yes, all the members of the society are."

"The one your father formed?" Rodney felt comfortable with the surroundings; friendly service, plush seats, they even had classical music playing in the background and the movie screen had curtains.

That's right, S.P.A.C.E. The Society for the Preservation of the Alhambra as a Cinematographic Emporium."

"The what?"

"SPACE," Gillian said with a rueful grin.

"Sounds good enough to me. You get the full treatment anyway. Is there any profit in it? Monetary?"

"Sometimes, but it's a registered non-profit organization. Most of the staff are volunteers. They get paid, but not much. The manager is a salaried employee. Any profits go straight back into the running of the place. What kind of ice cream do you like, by the way?"

"Choc ice. And if there is a net loss?"

"Daddy coughs up and his accountant uses it as a tax deduction. The ice cream girl comes round in the intermission."

"It must be nice to be rich, Gillian."

Our heroine became quiet and looked away. "It can also be a bit of a burden, Rodney," she muttered.

Rodney was about to ask her what was the matter but, before he could, the background music picked up in volume. The lights dimmed further, the music diminished and the curtains parted. The show was about to begin. Instead of speaking, Rodney put his arm around Gillian. She cuddled closer in response, her breath warm in his ear. He turned his face towards hers and their lips met, tentatively at first then becoming more passionate. He put his right hand to her slim waist and she, her left hand to caress his neck. Gillian's lips parted slightly; Rodney's pulse started to pound in his ears and he knew, this time he was in love... for real!

After the movie, the happy couple drove back to Occles-Leigh. Our heroine, however, would not be driven up to the Manor House. She told Rodney that she needed the walk. Therefore, he stopped in the lane at the bottom of the drive and, taking his sweetheart in both arms, kissed her amorously on the mouth.

They exchanged a few 'Oh, Rodneys' and 'Oh, Gillians' before she managed to pry herself loose. "I'll meet you at 'Rhodas' tomorrow for lunch," she promised, getting out of the car.

"Just after twelve?"

"Yes." She kissed him lightly on the cheek then turned away.

Rodney watched her scrunch up the gravel drive until she was out of sight. He then re-started his 1100 in order to wend his way back to the hotel. Back to the hotel and his lonely bed.

The Heiress and the Banker
Chapter Five
In Which 'ilda Says Her Piece

Breakfast the following morning. Mrs. Braithewaite, in her usual pinny and curlers, stands in the kitchen doorway.

"I've just bethowt mesen."

"What?" The local dialect was still a little beyond Rodney's ken.

"It just popped into me 'ead when I was gettin' the breakfast things ready," 'ilda said. "'ow's that boss o' yours? Samuel. I've not seen 'ide nor 'air o' 'im lately. 'appen 'e's mentioned me to you?"

"He did tell me that you and he are old friends," he said, wondering how come Mrs. Braithewaite would suddenly be bethowting herself of him.

"Aye, that's right. More so since my poor Norman passed away. Still, I'll not trouble you with that. 'ow d'ya want your sausage done, by the way? Fried or grilled?"

"Either way, 'ilda. I'm not too bothered as long as it's a meaty one."

Mrs. Braithewaite disappeared into the kitchen momentarily, then popped her head around the door jamb. "I've always liked 'em meaty mesenn," she said, with a girlish laugh.

About five minutes later, she re-appeared, bringing the fry-up into the dining room. There was an extra tea mug on the tray.

"There y'are, love," she said, placing Rodney's breakfast in front of him. "Eat 'earty." She put the tray aside, sat down and poured herself a cuppa. "I'll 'ave one with you this morning, if you don't mind, Rodney."

She held the pot over Rodney's mug and poured him a fresh cup.

"'ow was your night out at th' pictures?" she said casually. She covered the teapot with the cosey. "Was it a good filum?"

"James Bond, 'ilda." Rodney shoved a generous portion of sausage and egg into his mouth, then reached for the H.P. Sauce. "Can't fail," he mumbled.

"I liked that other chap better mesenn… Sheen Connery."

Our hero nodded, his cheeks bulging.

"Did your date enjoy it? Or are you goin' to tell old 'ilda that a good lookin' young chap like yerself went on 'is Jack Jones?"

"No, I didn't go by myself, 'ilda," he said, between chews. "And yes, my date enjoyed it. She's a real James Bond fan."

Mrs. Braithewaite took a good pull of her tea then homed in.

"Rodney, love, it's none o' my business o' course, but were it the Colonel's daughter you was out with last night? Young Gillian?"

"It was, yes. I don't know, 'ilda, I've only been here two days and I think I've already fallen in love. It's fate, must be." He gave the sauce bottle a good shake, thumped the bottom and poured a great dollop over his baked beans.

"I 'ad a feelin' that it was Miss Gillian. It was 'er you was askin' about yesterdee morning, I knew it was. I saw 'er go through the bar like that. Enough to make any man's 'ead turn."

Mrs. Braithewaite took another gulp of tea, then went on. "It's not my place to say owt, I know, and I hope you're not offended."

Rodney forked up a load of sausage and beans, meanwhile, 'ilda ploughed on.

"Miss Gillian is a different class of people than me and you, Rodney. I dare say as she's a nice girl, but you don't know what surprises she might 'ave in store. And she's not without friends of her own sort. Don't go jumpin' in wi' both feet, that's all I'm sayin'. You're a nice lad, Rodney, a credit to your mother. She must be very proud of you and I'm takin' the liberty of speakin' for 'er. Don't go gettin' 'urt, that's all I'm sayin'. 'ave a care." Then, being one of those ladies who seem to be in possession of an asbestos lined throat, she downed the remainder of her tea in one gulp. After which, she stood up, turned on her heel and was gone.

Rodney watched her disappear into the kitchen, shrugged again then turned back to the business of polishing off his breakfast.

A few minutes later, he was crossing the car park. He pulled his collar up against the early morning chill. The sky was overcast, a brisk wind blowing out of the north. Rodney shivered. He could barely wait for lunch time and the girl of his dreams.

≈ ≈ ≈ ≈ ≈

Back in the kitchen, Mrs. Braithewaite submerged the frying pan under a mass of soapy bubbles, brow furrowed and lips compressed. She had seen Gillian with Young Ponsomby-Smythe and knew of his plans. Girls could be fickle, as well she knew, and she didn't want to see her guest getting hurt. She gave the frying pan a good rubbing with the scouring pad. Duty done, she wouldn't mention the matter to Rodney again. She had said her piece and that was that.

≈ ≈ ≈ ≈ ≈

Gillian Brereton-Holbeck stomped into the house by the back way. She rubbed her hands briskly. What a change from the day before. Breakfast would not be on the verandah today. Pulling off her hiking boots, she decided she would enjoy the cozy atmosphere of breakfast in the kitchen, rather than face the snooty butler and the Morning Room. Gillian liked the down to Earth company of the cook and had not paid her a visit for a while. This morning seemed the ideal time.

"Good morning, Mrs. Morgan," Gillian said brightly on entering the cook's domain. She had showered and changed for the day. "Is there any tea on the go?"

"That there be, Miss Gillian, that there be. I'll get 'ee a cup."

The cook, originally from Cornwall, had moved north with her husband. He was a tin-basher at a nearby motor manufacturer's.

"Would 'ee like some breakfast as well, Miss?"

"Oh, yes please, Mrs. Morgan. I'm famished."

"'ere's your tea, Miss. I'll do 'ee bacon 'n' eggs. It'll be a few minutes."

Just then, Smithers marched importantly into the kitchen, nose ceilingward.

"Another kipper for Himself, Mefanway. I swear he'll be looking like one soon... Oh, sorry, Miss Gillian." He placed his silver tray on the kitchen counter. "Will you be present in the Morning Room today, Miss?"

"No, not today, Smithers." She smiled. "Relax! We're in the kitchen now. Nobody here but us chickens." Gillian sat down on a stool, back to the counter.

"As you say, Miss Gillian." Smithers turned his attention back to the cook who handed him the Colonel's third kipper.

"Thank you, Mefanway," he said, picking up his tray. With a nod in Gillian's direction, he turned on his heel and left.

Gillian giggled, her hands cupped around her mug of tea.

"Now you know he doesn't like to be teased, young lady," the cook said. "Very professional is Harold Smithers."

"I know, but sometimes I can't help myself. He can be so pompous."

"I'll not comment on that, Miss. I'll just get on with me cookin'."

About ten minutes later, Mrs. Morgan handed Gillian her breakfast. "There y'are, Miss." She picked up Gillian's empty tea mug. "I'll get 'ee a refill of tea…"

The cook gasped, her dark eyes popping as she stared into the bottom of the mug.

"What is it, Mrs. Morgan." Gillian put her breakfast on the counter top and got to her feet. "Have you seen something awful?"

"It be nothing, Miss Gillian," the cook replied, hastily rinsing the mug under the kitchen tap. She seemed half afraid that the young mistress of the house would read the portents for herself.

"'ee tea leaves don't speak to old Mefanway this mornin'."

"But…?"

"It be nothin', Miss Gillian. Just a bit of wind that's all." The cook rubbed her side. "You get on with your breakfast afore it goes cold. I've got plenty to do today, then there's 'im at 'ome later on and 'e won't be denied you know, oh, no, not 'im." Mrs. Morgan scurried about the kitchen. "I'm a busy woman I am, oh, yes, so you'll 'ave to excuse me now."

Gillian picked up her knife and fork. "What has that woman seen now?" she thought.

She was still in pensive mood at mid-day when she sat down for lunch with Rodney. Mefanway Morgan had an uncanny gift of the second sight when it came to the reading of the cups, and Gillian knew it. She had definitely seen something unpleasant. Still, quizzing the cook would be a bit like interrogating the back door. Gillian would gain nothing but frustration.

"Penny for them?"

"Sorry?"

"Your thoughts. A penny for your thoughts."

"Oh, sorry, Rodney, I was miles away." She reached out to touch his hand. "Take no notice of me."

"There y'are, ducks. Two pasties, two sausage rolls and pot of tea for two," quoth 'Little Rhoda'. "Turned out nice again 'asn't hit?'". She waited while the pair released each others hands, fingertips lingering momentarily. She then placed their dinner tray on the table.

"Turned out very nice," Rodney said. "After such a poor start as well." He dragged out his wallet, eyeing up the bill.

"Sorry about th' price increase, but you know 'ow things are these days. I blame all them American Sputniks, I do. Messin' th' weather up and everything they are, you mark my words. As if we 'aven't got enough problems already."

Rodney handed her a fifty pence piece. "Keep the change, Rhoda," he said. "Service with a smile is always appreciated."

"Oh, er, thank you, I'm sure," Rhoda said, a puzzled look on her face. She shrugged, pocketed the coin and went on her way.

"Not being facetious are we, Rodney?" Gillian said.

"I just appreciate service with a smile, that's all, Gillian." He picked up one of the sausage rolls. "Dig in."

Gillian helped herself to a pastie. "Speaking as a banker," she said. "What is your opinion on the American space programme, their use of Russian Sputniks and the effect it all has on the weather and inflation in Britain?"

"I don't have one," Rodney laughed. "How was your morning?"

"Spent the time cleaning the back room. Rebecca was complaining about her chilblains, asked me how my M.G. was running and 'Didn't her Rowena's 'enry 'ave one once?' I told her that Rowena's Henry might have had one once, but I don't and my Triumph is running nicely. Waste of time though. She still thinks it's an M.G."

"Must be annoying."

"A little. Where's the tart with the tart, by the way?"

"Tart with the tart?"

"You know, 'Little Miss Smith'. I saw how you looked at her yesterday… no… don't deny it. Admit you're human. She's a little tart and you can't keep your eyes off her."

Rodney swallowed the last remnants of his sausage roll.

"Gillian, you're the only woman I can't keep my eyes off," he said. "'Little Miss Smith' may well be attractive, and she is certainly an exhibitionist, but she's not my type. She's filling in for one of the tellers today anyway. Weren't hoping to see her, were you?"

"Well," Gillian said with a giggle. "It would be interesting to see how she goes about eating one of these." She picked up the other sausage roll. "What a performance yesterday with the chocolate éclair. I picked one up after work and tried eating it her way in front of the dresser mirror. Couldn't stop laughing at myself."

Rodney had set about eating his pastie. "Why would you do that?" he mumbled.

"I saw how you looked at her yesterday," Gillian said quietly.

Rodney swallowed hard. "She's just one of the staff, Gillian. All this talk of Roxanne Smith and chocolate éclairs. How come you work at the Charity Shop anyway?" he said. "Not for the money, obviously."

"Charity! The regular girl is away this week and I thought that it would be nice to make myself useful. What it must be to be an ordinary girl and have a job to go to. Not to have to listen to 'Miss Gillian' this and 'Miss Gillian' that. I sometimes think that I would be better off if my parents weren't so wealthy. Then there's my twenty-first birthday coming up and… Don't roll your eyes at me like that, Rodney. Wealth can be a burden, you've no idea."

"There's worse things to be than rich," Rodney said.

Gillian picked up the teapot and started to pour. "That's part of the problem, Rodney. How do I tell if you, for instance, are genuinely interested in me? Or is it the money?"

"Gillian, how could you think that? I fell in love with you at first sight. Yesterday, I had no idea you were wealthy and a heiress and now it makes no difference."

"Ohhh!" Gillian jumped out of her seat. The cup she had been filling was overflowing, the table awash with tea.

"'ere y'are! I'll see to that, ducks." 'Big Rhoda' slapped an oversized dishcloth into the middle of the spillage. She had emerged, like a charging rhino, from behind the counter at the first sign of trouble. "There we are!" A few deft strokes with a well-developed forearm and all was well.

"Oh, Rhoda… I don't know what…"

"Never you mind, ducks. Accidents 'appen. I'll get you a fresh pot. You and your chap sit tight."

Our heroine resumed her seat, Rodney quickly following suit.

"I feel so…"

"Forget it. She's quick for a big un."

"Yes." Gillian's eyes began to sparkle again, a smile forming on her lips. "What was it you were saying, Blue-Eyes?"

"Oh, er, what was it now?" Rodney rubbed his chin thoughtfully.

Gillian laughed. He had fallen in love with her at first sight. Her young heart leapt.

The second pot of tea was delivered and dispatched without incident. Then, lunch being over, our happy pair left the bakery hand in hand.

Gillian asked Rodney to drop into the Charity Shop after work as there was something special she had to show him. Rodney said he would. After a brief but passionate kiss, they parted company for the remainder of the afternoon.

Our hero made his way back to the bank on the same side of the street as 'Rhodas' and, as he passed the Alhambra, Avonlea's came into view on the other side. He could see Roxanne outside the building in the now bright sunshine. She was standing on the footpath with her left foot on the bottom step, her skirt pulled back. She kept trying to flip her hair out of her eyes while trying to adjust something at the top of her thigh.

"Suspenders?" Rodney thought, with a sharp intake of breath. "A garter belt?" He quickened his pace.

Our hero was not the only witness to this entrancing little scene. Outside the 'White Boar', a gang of roughly clad young fellows, ale pots in hand, stood around to gawp and gape. They were in uproar, wolf whistling, cheering and shouting.

"Gerrem off!"

"Drop 'em, blossom!"

"Will ya risk it for a biscuit?"

"Are ya willin' for a shillin'?" a piping voice called out.

Meanwhile, Miss Smith carried on as if she hadn't noticed any of this and, as Rodney approached, she flipped her skirt back into place. As if by way of an encore, she started to adjust her other stocking.

Our hero crossed the street and glared balefully at the ruffians outside the pub. They took not one blind bit of notice of him.

Roxanne flipped her skirt back into place again and stood back from the steps. She gave Rodney a joyful smile. "Hello, Mister Watkinson. Did you have a nice lunch?"

The lads down the street drifted back into the pub, the show now being over.

"Hardly the proper behaviour for an Avonlea's employee, Miss Smith. Would you say that that is the proper way to behave on the High Street around here?"

"Certainly not, Mister Watkinson, but don't worry. They don't work for Avonlea's, they're from the sawmill down Broome's Lane."

Rodney opened his mouth but...

"See you later, Sweety," Roxanne chirped. Then, hem of her skirt dancing tantalizingly, she set off down the street.

Our hero watched her go, he could not help himself. Little tart, Gillian had called her. Well, maybe so, but he couldn't help but to admire her style. He would have to get her to tone down her appearance though, hardly the proper thing for Avonlea's at all.

He decided he would discuss the dress code with her later in the week, give himself time to get more of a feel for his new position.

Miss Smith now out of sight, Rodney pulled his tie out of his pocket and went up the steps to the bank's front door. It would be a long afternoon 'til he could see Gillian again.

At the Charity Shop, Gillian took the Saville Row suit (late of the Colonel's wardrobe) and draped it over a chair in the back room. She had the idea that, with a bit of running in, it would look good on her Rodney. Her own feelings on the matter apart, she thought he really should have at least one good suit if she intended to present him at the Manor House. And Gillian did intend to present him.

≈ ≈ ≈ ≈ ≈

Around half-past-four that afternoon, Rodney arrived. The two older ladies eyed him up and twittered to each other quietly.

"Mmm! Nice chap!" Rebecca said.

"Yesss! Where was he when I was single?"

"When you were single?"

Gillian smiled from ear to ear. She took hold of Rodney's hand and led him to the back room.

"Try this on," she said, without pre-amble.

Rodney removed his jacket and hung it over the chair back, tie already stuffed into a pocket. Gillian held the Saville Row suit jacket while Rodney slipped his arms into the sleeves. On the Colonel it refused to meet in the middle; on Rodney it was double-breasted.

"I thought it would be nice for special occasions," Gillian said.

"Yes… Like when the circus comes to town. Or maybe I could gain three or four stone?"

"Oh, you silly billy. Rowena can run it in for you. It will be made to measure by the time she has finished with it. It's all been arranged."

"That's right," Rowena agreed, entering the room with her sister in tow. "Five pounds and you can pick it up next Monday. We'll trust you for the fiver. Pay up whenever you can spare it."

"Can't say no to that," Rodney said. He removed the jacket and reached for his own.

"I'll measure you up now shall I?" Rowena said.

"Might as well. I'm standing here anyway."

"We might as well 'ave a brew then," Rebecca said, filling the hard working kettle. "'as our Gillian taken you for a ride in 'er M.G. yet, Rodney?"

Gillian rolled her eyes as Rodney replied, "Not yet, but soon I hope." He caught our heroine's eye.

"It's a Triumph," she mouthed, then, "Tomorrow night, if you like. I can't see you tonight, prior arrangements I'm afraid."

"That's all right." Rodney lifted his arms to allow Rowena to wrap the tape measure around his chest. "And I would like a ride in your M.G.," he smirked.

"Not if you keep that up."

"Triumph?"

"Seven o' clock tomorrow night. I'll pick you up at the hotel." Gillian went to help Rebecca with the tea, leaving Rowena to her measuring which, as it turned out, was taking overly long.

"Come on, our Rowena. Are you goin' to take all night? You've measured 'is inside leg three times already. What's the to-do? Come and 'ave a cup o' tea wi' us. It's gettin' cowd."

"Oh, all right," Rowena snapped. She rolled her tape measure up. "There's no need to go on about it." She smiled at Rodney. "All right, love, I've finished for now. I might 'ave to measure you up again later in th' week if that's all right with you?"

"Whatever you think is necessary," Rodney replied. He accepted a cuppa from Gillian, then the pair stood together sipping tea and allowed the sisters the semi-privacy of the table.

"By the way, Gillian, I'll be going down the Smoke this weekend," Rodney said.

"Oh? So soon?"

"'fraid so. I have some loose ends to tie up and then there's my mum. I want to make sure she's all right."

"That's very sweet of you, Rodney, worrying about your mum like that. Is she very old?"

"Not really, I suppose, but I have to keep my eye on her."

"Mmm! I suspect it is more the other way around, but if that's your story…"

"I'd better stick to it? I have Friday off anyway, so I'll be leaving Thursday straight after work."

"I see. I'll count the minutes while you're away, Blue-Eyes."

"The seconds myself…"

Ther eyes met; they sighed.

With an effort of will, Rodney dragged himself away and walked over to the sink, drank the remainder of his tea, swilled the cup out and placed it on the counter.

"Thanks for the hospitality, ladies," he said. "But I have to be on my way."

"Oh, any time, love," the sisters replied in chorus.

"Don't forget about the suit, young man," Rowena trilled as he stepped into the passageway, Gillian at his side.

"Oh, to be young again, our Rebecca…"

"…and in love, our Rowena… and in love…"

"I think you've scored a hit there, Rodney," Gillian giggled. She put one arm around his waist as the sisters' voices faded into the distance.

"Let Gillian know if you want to measure my inside leg again," Rodney called out.

"Oh, you…"

Once outside and under the bright sun of the afternoon, Gillian asked, "Lunch tomorrow?"

"Yes, usual time." He pulled her towards him, their lips met.

Gillian responded feverishly to his passionate kisses until (to the disappointment of several passers-by) they reluctantly broke their embrace. Rodney then set off in the direction of the 'White Boar' and his waiting car. He turned once; Gillian blew him a kiss, then went back to the relative gloom of the Charity Shop to take care of the chores.

After washing up the tea things and putting them away, Gillian was ready to leave. "I'll see you in the morning," she called out as she went to the door.

"All right, love…"

"We won't be long ourselves…"

"Tarra, love," both sisters called out together.

By the time the older ladies had emerged from the shop, our heroine was waiting to pull out into Wheelock Street.

As she waited for a space in the slow moving traffic, she heard Rebecca and Rowena talking.

"Oh, look, our Rowena! There's nowt like an M.G. with the top down. Why your 'enry got rid of 'is I'll never know."

"Cheeky bugger said it was 'cos 'e cuddna get mae into th' back seat, if you must know."

"Oh, aye! A good back seat comes in 'andy sometimes. It was either that or th' back row of th' pictures for me and our Arthur."

They were still cackling with laughter as Gillian, hand raised in salute, pulled away towards Nantwich Road.

"Use your imaginations, girls," she muttered, glancing at them in the rearview mirror. "There's more in life than a back seat, in a car or at the pictures."

Pulling out of the town's speed limit, Gillian opened the TR up. It was a joy to be alive! Rodney of the Oh-So-Blue-Eyes had shown her that.

The Heiress and the Banker
Chapter Six
Teatime

By the time that Gillian reached Occles-Leigh, Roxanne Smith was at home. She lived in one of the terraced houses of the avenues with her mam and her older sister. She tucked into her tea of bacon and fried tomatoes, tight fitting jeans and a light blue halter top being her choice of clothing for the evening.

"Our Roxanne was teasin' th' lads again at dinner time, mam."

"Shurrup, our Andrea. You know nowt about it. Anyway, it's none o' your business is it?"

"You should 'ave seen 'er, mam. I come out o' th' paper shop to see what the commotion was about outside o' th' 'White Boar' and there's our Roxy with 'er skirt 'round 'er waist. Adjustin' 'er suspenders she was. Th' lads from th' sawmill were in uproar."

"Shurrup!" Roxanne hissed.

"Why don't you just become a stripper, Roxy? You'd be good on th' stage and it would be safer than performin' on th' street. You'd make money at it as well… and maybe a little extra on th' side."

"Get on wi' your tea an' leave th' lass alone," Mother Smith cut in. "She's a woman grown, our Andrea and'll do as 'er pleases." She bent her head back over her plate. "'appen as 'er'll learn 'er lesson afore too much longer," she muttered.

"If th' wind changes you'll stick like that," Andrea said.

Roxanne pulled her tongue back into her mouth and sniffed. She picked up a slice of bread, took a bite, then cut into a piece of bacon.

"D'ya fancy goin' to 'Cool Cat's on Satdee night, our Roxy? We could eye up some talent."

"Yeah, all right," Roxanne said, between chews. "Shall we wear our garters belts and that? Give th' lads an eyeful?"

"Well, I wouldn't mind." Andrea took the last slice of bread and mopped it around her plate with her fork. "I've better legs than you any day o' th' week."

"We'll see about that. Do you remember Blackpool Pier last summer?"

"I do an' all!" Andrea replied. They both started to giggle. "We 'ad them lad's eyes poppin'. Wear your underdrawers this Satdee night though, our Roxy. I won't get a look in, else."

"What I wear under me skirt is nobody's business but me own. Come to think of it, I might just wear me scarlet red uns."

"That's your colour that is, our Roxy, scarlet red."

The girls went quiet. Meanwhile, Mother Smith sat with tea cup in hand, a faraway look on her face. She also remembered Blackpool Pier, but not last summer. She remembered Blackpool Pier (or, more precisely, the golden sands underneath it) during that long hot summer of 1953. Andrea had been born the following spring. Her ears perked up. The girls had finished eating and were gossiping again.

"…Tommy Boyle. 'e was in th' paper shop today askin' about you. Fancies you like mad 'e does. You could do worse." Andrea smirked, "I've 'eard it said as 'e gives good measure, if you know what I mean, our Roxy."

Mother Smith got up from the table. "Good measure? Whatever will you girls say next?" She had heard enough. "I'm goin' watch th' six o' clock news. See as you wash up, you two." She started for the living room.

"All right, mam," Andrea answered, pouring herself more tea.

Roxanne, meanwhile, had gone red in the face. She too had heard that he gave good measure, and she didn't like the thought of it. It made her nervous. "I'm not interested in Tommy Boyle, thank you very much, Andrea," she stated in a low but firm voice.

"Not interested? Why ever not?"

"I'm savin' meself, if you must know."

"Savin' yourself? The way you go on? Don't tell me that you're just a tease, our Roxy? If you'd any sense, you'd let me give the word to Tommy…"

"No!"

Andrea's eyes lit up. "It's that Cockney bank manager, isn't it? You're savin' yourself for 'im." She got to her feet. "You don't stand a chance there. Miss Rich Britches 'as got 'im wrapped round 'er little finger from what I 'ear. Anyway, 'elp us clear the table."

Roxanne had already sprung to her feet. She slammed her cup down onto the table's worn top.

"'e's not a Cockney! e's not the bank manager!" She glared at her sister. "And 'e 'asn't married 'er yet." She strode out of the kitchen. "You can wash up by yourself." The door slammed. "I'm goin' watch th' news with me mam."

"Sorry I spoke, I'm sure," her sister muttered, then, "Don't worry, Tommy. I'll bring 'er round for you." She went about her kitchen duties with renewed vigour.

≈ ≈ ≈ ≈ ≈

At the Manor House, the Brereton-Holbeck's had seated themselves for dinner. This meal being set for eighteen hundred hours precisely, care of the Colonel. Although there was only the family present, proper attire had to be worn.

"Discipline!" the Colonel was fond of saying. "Separates the civilized from the savage, what?"

At the moment we join this gentile scene, Smithers is making his haughty way to the kitchen with the used soup dishes. He will return (smugly) with the main course, duck a la orange, shortly. In the interval between courses the Colonel, seated at 'his' head of the table, said casually, "By the way, Gillian my petal, there was a phone call for you this afternoon. Young Cedric. Said he'd pick you up at eight for the dance on Saturday night. I took the liberty of inviting the chap to come early enough to join us for dinner. I hope that that is to your liking, my petal?"

"Botheration!" Gillian muttered.

"What's that, my sweet?" The Colonel cupped a hand to one ear.

"Oh, nothing, daddy. That arrangement will be fine."

"Dashed good fellow is young Cedric," the Colonel went on. "A fine catch for you, my girl. He'll inherit the title and Ponsomby Towers when that time comes. A fine catch. Well, you're a sensible girl, Gillian and I'm sure you don't intend becoming an old maid…"

"That's quite enough matchmaking, Cuthbert, thank you!" Her Ladyship said archly from the head of the table. She regarded her husband with compressed lips.

"I was just saying, my dear, what a sensible young lady Gillian is. Young Cedric and all…"

The young lady in question was no longer listening. She sat with furrowed brow, her eyes downcast. "Sensible indeed? Look where sensible has got me. Almost twenty-one years old and still a maiden." Her expression changed. Now she gazed wistfully at the ceiling. "Perhaps Rodney Blue-Eyes can help me change some of that," she thought. "Perhaps I should try being a bit less sensible."

The Heiress and the Banker
Chapter Seven
A Ride in the Woods

Our hero had waited patiently outside the 'Occles-Leigh Arms Hotel' for his date to arrive. Now he lifted his rump from the front wing of his 1100, the staccato bark of the TR's exhaust carried to him on the light breeze. Gillian pulled into the car park and he broke into a trot. "Hi!" he called out. Zipping up his leather jacket, he made his way to where she had come to a stop.

"You'll need that jacket tonight," Gillian said. "Could get breezy."

Gillian herself was wearing a black windproof jacket over a lightweight sweater. Her hair was tied back in the same fashion as on Monday morning. As Rodney climbed into the roadster, she leaned towards him for a quick kiss. Rodney noticed that she wore a black knee length skirt tonight, a pleated skirt, together with her white socks and sandals. As their lips met, Rodney (quite unconsciously) placed one hand on her knee. Gillian's initial reaction had been to pull him closer; now she pushed him gently away. "Buckle up!" she said, her eyes twinkling. "Full moon later on and we, like the night, are young."

"Sounds promising," Rodney said. He snapped his seat belt together with a thunk.

Mrs. Braithewaite walked slowly round from the back of the pub. She watched as the TR5 swept out onto the road to barrel off in the direction of Nantwich. A smile lit up her time-worn face.

"Oh, to be young and in love!" she said aloud.

Her lips pursed as she remembered Gillian's other young man. How it would all end, she didn't know, but she had tried to warn Rodney. She had done her bit.

"Monty? What are you doin' out 'ere?"

The old dog had mopesed along after her and now sat faithfully at her feet. "Come on," she said. "Let's go get you somethin' to drink shall we?" The dog lifted himself to his all fours and followed her back to the yard.

≈ ≈ ≈ ≈ ≈

Gillian had driven the car quite hard, the 'Occles Leigh Arms Hotel' now being far behind them. Conversation had been kept to a minimum while she and Rodney enjoyed the wind-rushing, engine bellowing, exhaust barking ride. It was quite a ride as well, but our heroine did not open the TR up to anywhere near full throttle until they were approaching Tarvinley.

"Do you fancy a cup of tea?" she shouted in Rodney's ear.

The car slowed as they came to a junction. Rodney nodded, although he would have thought more of a pint of ale.

"O.K. Hang on!" Gillian yelled. She pulled out onto the Chester by-pass and floored the throttle, only backing off as she went through the gears. Rodney felt himself pushed into his seat at every up-change until, wind driven tears lashing from the corners of his eyes, he glanced at the speedometer. He looked away and looked again, but too late to confirm what he had seen registered there. Gillian was slowing the car down, dropping to third, then second gear as the 'Windy Ridge Café' came into view on their left.

"Are you sure you're not related to Jackie Stewart?" Rodney said.

"Only in spirit." Gillian pulled the car into the café's car park, came to a stop and shut the engine off.

"Come on!" she said. "They do a good brew here." She was out of the car and striding towards the café while Rodney was still wrestling with his seat belt. As he trotted to catch up with her, he noticed that the hem of Roxanne's skirt was not the only one capable of dancing tantalizingly.

"I can see why they call it 'Windy Ridge'," he said as he drew alongside, head bowed to the wind.

"Yes! It is a bit exposed."

The café stood on a west facing ridge at the top of a long hill. The dual carriageway of the Chester by-pass ran past the north side and the road back in to the village of Tarvinley by the south.

"It's one of my favourite stops, this," Gillian said. "I went to boarding school here."

"After you, Madam!" Rodney held the door and ushered Gillian into the cosy interior of the café.

"Yes, that seems like a long time ago now," Gillian went on. "'Felicity Fontleroy's School for Young Ladies'. Felicity's Fillies they used to call us. We used to get up to all sorts of pranks. Oh, look, take a table by the window. I won't be long. Have to powder my nose."

Rodney watched as she hurried off to the ladies'. He wondered where all the bobbies were tonight. He was sure that, if he drove like she did, they'd lock him up and throw away the key.

"Table for two, is it, love?"

"Yes. By the window, please."

The waitress showed him to a window seat. Once seated, he asked for a pot of tea for two. He then removed his leather jacket and draped it over the chair back. After the wind-blown ride, the café seemed hot.

They were lingering over their second cup of tea, gazing into each others eyes, when Gillian suddenly said, "Do you have any other girlfriends, Rodney? Tucked away in London, perhaps?"

Our hero was taken aback. "Why no, Gillian. Why would you think it? There are women I am friends with, but no-one special." He paused. "You're my one and only, my dream come true."

"But not the first girlfriend you have ever had?"

"Well, I have had girlfriends prior to meeting you…"

"And?" Gillian sipped her tea.

"And I love you."

Gillian smiled longingly, gazing into his eyes. "Tell me of your past, Kimbo Savvy. I would like to know."

Rodney drank the remainder of his tea, then placed his cup on the saucer.

"A couple of years ago, I was engaged to a girl. Deborah her name was. We were going to get married."

"Of course. Go on."

"A week before the wedding was to take place, I found out that she had been sleeping with my cousin."

"Oh, no! How awful!" Gillian gasped. "Your cousin. Did you catch them… at it… you know?"

"Nothing like that. My cousin told me. Couldn't stand the deception any longer."

"Oh, Rodney! It must have been awful for you. I'm sorry I made you tell me now."

"I got over it. It was a terrible shock at the time though."

"Did you and this cousin of yours get into fisticuffs over it?"

"Fisti whats?"

Gillian rolled her sleeves up and made like she was boxing.

"Fisticuffs! Did you thump him?"

Rodney looked sheepish. "You don't understand, Gillian. I wasn't brought up to thump girls."

"Girls?" Gillian slipped her sleeves back into place.

"Yes, girls. Deborah had been sleeping with my cousin Jemima. I could never hit Jemima, no matter what she had done."

"Your cousin Jemima?" Gillian spluttered. "Oh, I'm sorry, Rodney. I know it's not funny…"

"Gillian, it's hilarious." Rodney got to his feet. "Jemima did me a favour. She's welcome to what she's got. I've found someone much, much better! Come on, don't hang about with your mouth open, let's go."

While Rodney shrugged into his leather jacket, Gillian tucked a pound note under her saucer. Enough to pay for the pot of tea and allow for an ample tip.

After their brief respite at the Windy Ridge, Gillian drove at a more moderate pace back along the Chester by-pass. They were going in the direction of North Wilderspool. After several miles, she turned the car left and onto a small side road.

"I'll take you through Delamere Woods," she shouted above the wind-rush.

Rodney nodded. She could take him wherever she liked as far as he was concerned; as long as they were together, he was happy.

They poodled along at about forty miles an hour, enjoying the scenery and wind in their hair. After a while, they came to a smaller road, which Gillian wheeled the car onto. This road was narrow, winding and was flanked on both sides by tall evergreens.

"Delamere Woods," she said, with a sweep of a hand.

Rodney noticed that there were lay-bys every half mile or so and, not surprisingly, Gillian pulled over and stopped the car in one of these. She shut the engine off; no sound now apart from the rustling of the trees and evening birdsong. They both sat back and looked at the sky. A pink glow was visible to the west and the first stars of evening beginning to appear.

"Another nice day tomorrow by the looks of things," Gillian said.

"Yes," Rodney agreed, turning to caress her about the waist.

"Red sky at night…" he whispered. They were lost in the depths of each others eyes.

"…Sailors' delight!" Gillian finished. As their lips met, Rodney's hand once again alighted on her knee.

"Wait!"

"What now?"

Gillian gently pushed him back into his seat. "You'll see," she whispered.

The TR's engine barked into life and Gillian wheeled the Triumph back onto the narrow road.

"Too busy along here."

Our hero started to whistle a happy tune, but stopped himself.

"Not a change of heart then," he thought. He started to whistle again. He just couldn't help himself.

Gillian drove another mile or so until, slowing down, she turned through a gap between the trees. There was just enough room for the roadster to make headway along the woodland trail.

"This isn't very sensible, my girl," Gillian thought as she threaded her way along, then, "I know, oh, I know."

Half a mile further and the car nosed out into a little dell. "We sometimes used to camp here when I was at Felicity Fontleroy's," Gillian explained as she pulled to a stop. "It's quite invisible from the road and a chance passer-by wouldn't know it was here. Come on. Take your shoes and socks off." She shut the engine off and opened her door. Turning sideways in her seat, she took off her sandals and socks.

With a shrug, Rodney followed suit. "What do you have in mind? Getting back to nature are we?"

"Something like that!" Gillian walked round to his side of the car. She held out a hand; Rodney took it in his and got to his feet.

"We're going to walk barefoot through the woods," Gillian said. "You'll enjoy it. You'll see."

To Rodney's surprise, he did enjoy it. The forest floor had a sensuous feel between his toes and he found the smell of spruce and pine to be invigourating.

The wind had begun to moan softly through the tall trees and the sun had set by the time they returned to the car. The full moon, as promised by Gillian, was rising above the tops of the trees. Our hero and heroine sat against the front of the TR's bonnet gazing up at the myriad stars.

"It's a beautiful night," Rodney said.

"Yes!" Gillian breathed, cuddling closer. She shivered slightly, though the wind was warm.

"You're beautiful, Gillian." Rodney turned his face towards hers. "More beautiful than the stars above; more haunting than a golden sunset over a faraway sea…"

"Shussh!"

Rodney moved her finger away from his lips. He was lost in the fathomless deeps of her eyes as he murmured, "I love you, Gillian… I love you!"

A sigh escaped from Gillian's lips as their mouths met hungrily. She did not resist as Rodney laid her down on the bonnet of the TR. It was a beautiful night and she had a wonderful view of the stars. She did not think of England once as nature took its age-old course there in the ancient woods of Delamere.

The moon looked serenely on; the wind sighed through the tree tops; the sounds of a busy day replaced by those of a velvet night. Our happy couple remained where they were, locked in passionate ecstasy; united in love's sweet fulfillment.

The Heiress and the Banker
Chapter Eight
The Morning After the Night Before

Thursday morning and Rodney was in fine fettle; as well indeed he might be. He had packed a change of clothes in a suitcase for his weekend in London, singing all the while, "Everything's going my way…" Mrs. Braithewaite had even given him an extra sausage that morning.

"Enjoy your weekend, Rodney and give my regards to your mam," she had called out as he left.

"I'll try my best, 'ilda, don't you worry," Rodney replied, dumping his suitcase into the back of his car. "I'll see you Sunday night."

Mrs. Braithewaite waved as he drove off. "'e must 'ave 'ad a good night out last night," she said to herself. "See you Sunday night and you say 'ello to Sammy for me!" she shouted. She plodded back into the yard thinking once again, "What is must be to be young and in love!"

Rodney's high spirits lasted all morning. He had been whistling most of the time and had asked Roxanne to be in his office at 1:30 P.M. for a meeting.

"It's about office attire, Miss Smith," he informed her.

"Very well, Mister Watkinson," Roxanne replied with a bat of her eyelids. "I'll be there."

Work that morning had been a breeze and, before he knew it, it was time for our hero to meet his one and only heart's desire for lunch.

"Last night was wonderful," he confided once seated comfortably in 'Rhodas'.

"Don't start that, please!" Gillian snapped.

"Huh?"

"I've thought about nothing else all morning!" she said harshly.

"Yes, I've hardly thought of…"

"And I'd rather not discuss it here… If you don't mind!"

After making love in the woodland dell the night before, Gillian had wanted to discuss their future. Rodney, however, had fallen into a contented sleep in the warm cocoon of the car's interior.

"Gillian… I don't understand…"

"Rodney, don't, please. There are things I feel need to be discussed, but not here and now. Last night would have been the proper time."

Gillian had put the top up on the roadster for the drive back to Occles-Leigh; this for intimacies sake. Not so that our hero could sack out with a grin on his face like that of the proverbial Cheshire cat. There were things that she wanted to discuss all right, but not in a crowded café at high noon.

"Gillian, if it's something I've done…?"

She was no longer listening. Falling in love was all fine and dandy, but she had only known Rodney since Monday… and then on Wednesday night behaving like a… a… well! She now thought that she had acted rashly; on a car bonnet in the woods as well. Then he had the gall to fall asleep.

"It's obvious what he thinks of me," she thought glumly. Gillian felt that she had been used.

"'ere's your dinners, ducks," Rhoda said, placing the tray on the table. She looked knowingly from one to the other. "Aye, well," she muttered. "The path of true love never did run smooth."

"Thanks, Rhoda." Rodney forked out the money for the bill; Gillian insisted on paying her half.

He watched as Gillian picked at her food. He could not figure out what she was so upset about, other than it seemed to be something to do with the night before.

He mulled things over; he thought that there had to be a logical solution. Women liked to know you loved them; he did and had told her so, several times in fact. Therefore, she knew that he loved her. She had, in turn, demonstrated her love for him. Most ably in fact, inexperienced though she obviously was.

"Is everything all right, Gillian?" he asked, pouring the tea and hoping for a clue.

"Yes! It's just that… Oh, never mind. I expect I'll get over it."

Rodney rubbed his chin. He knew it had been her first time and wondered if she were unsure of her performance.

Poor Rodney! He had all the clues he needed; he had just never learned the language of the fairer sex. On top of that, he still imagined that emotional problems could be solved in a logical manner and so our hero blundered on.

"Gillian, I really enjoyed last night, if that is what is worrying you," he said. He leaned over the table towards her and lowered his voice. "You were great! A real pro."

Our heroine stared at him in disbelief; her lower lip started to quiver.

"Rodney Watkinson, that is it!" she blurted. "I am going back to the shop, if that is all you can think about." She jumped to her feet. "We'll sort this out when you get back from your precious Smoke. If you have any interest at all in me, that is."

"But… but…?"

"I'll meet you outside here on Monday. Perhaps by then you will have gotten over your selfishness."

"Huh?" Rodney got to his feet.

"No! Don't mind me. You finish your lunch…" Gillian put her handkerchief to her face. She turned and left almost at a run. The shelter of the Charity Shop was all she could think of.

Our hero became conscious of the silence that had fallen over the bakery just as conversation resumed. Normal routine was beginning to pick up once more as he sat down to a desultory meal. There was nothing for it. He would have to eat Gillian's share as well. What had gotten into her he did not know.

"Maybe 'That time of the month'?" he thought, chewing mechanically on a sausage roll.

His married colleagues in London had commented at length on that scenario often enough. Maybe that was what was at the root of all this? On top of last night as well.

Whatever! If Gillian wanted her own space to sort things out for herself, then so be it. He loved her and respected her as a person; he would not go chasing up the street after her. He would be back by Sunday night. He'd see her on Monday.

≈ ≈ ≈ ≈ ≈

By the time she ran headlong into the Charity Shop, Gillian was in a full flood of tears. She had behaved like a tart, she had decided. She was no better than that 'Jezebel' at the bank, the only difference being that she herself had been to finishing school.

As for Rodney, he could not possibly love her. If he did, he would surely have pursued her up the street and sorted things out there and then. Instead, he had just watched her go. She had been a good screw, he had as much as said so.

"'You were great!'" he had leered. "'A real pro.'" That was all she was, a good screw. Rodney had had what he wanted and then slept it off.

"I've only myself to blame," Gillian sobbed bitterly, her breath coming in ragged gasps. She turned and shut the door, leaning against its comforting solidity.

"Gillian, love? Good gracious, girl, whatever's the matter?"

Gillian turned and fell into the older woman's arms. "Oh, Rebecca, it's awful."

Rebecca had known that something was brewing all morning. It hadn't been just the tea either. "There, there, now," she soothed. "Was it 'im?"

"Oh, Rebecca, you don't understand. It's not his fault.

"I knew it, the rat! Knew it the minute I set eyes on 'im, I did. Men! Mmmph!"

"What's all the commotion about," Rowena asked. She came trotting down the passageway from the back room, tea cup in hand.

"It's 'im! That rat, Rodney." Rebecca gestured with her head for her sister to lock up shop.

"I knew it!" Rowena shrilled, locking the front door with a resounding click. "The rat!" hanging the 'Closed for Stocktaking, Sorry' sign in the window. "Knew it the minute I set eyes on 'im, I did. Men! Mmmph!"

"Come on, love," Rebecca soothed. "Our Rowena will make us a nice cup of tea. You can tell us all about it."

"Give 'em what they want then they leave you in the lurch. Men! Mmmph! All the same they are." Rowena screeched as she followed her sister and the distraught girl to the back room. "All the same!"

"It's not his fault," Gillian sobbed. "It's me. I'm just a…"

"No use tryin' to defend 'im," Rowena shrilled, filling the kettle. "'e's not worth it, believe you me. Not worth it at all. Isn't that right, our Rebecca?"

"Oh, that's right… Too right, that's right! Not worth it at all."

≈ ≈ ≈ ≈ ≈

Lunch over, Rodney hesitated outside the bakery. Should he go down to the Charity Shop and demand to know what was going on? Maybe tell Gillian that he loved her and was sorry for hurting her the way that he had? (Whatever it was that he had done) No! He would let her sort things out on her own, just as she had requested. That was only right. Besides, he had an appointment to keep with Miss Smith. Much as it irked him, he would have to put personal matters aside for the afternoon. He turned resolutely and strode off towards the bank.

≈ ≈ ≈ ≈ ≈

Miss Smith entered his office at 1:30 P.M. on the dot. Her leather skirt appeared to be even shorter than it had been that morning. "Well, at least she is punctual," Rodney allowed, with a glance at his watch.

"You wanted to see me?" Roxanne purred demurely.

"Yes! Take a seat, Miss Smith." He gestured to the chair opposite his.

Roxanne slinked over and pulled out the indicated chair, placing it a little further back from the desk than was necessary.

"I have to speak to you about the dress code, Miss Smith," Rodney said, using his best management voice.

"I see," Roxanne breathed. She sat down and crossed one leg over the other. "What would you like to know about it, Mister Watkinson?"

Rodney, ignoring her reply (and trying to ignore the hint of stocking top and garter belt) picked up a plasticized sheet. He proceeded to read from it.

"'Dress Code for all Avonlea's Bank Employees U.K.'," he began. He glanced at his assistant. "I'll read you the relevant section, Miss Smith."

"I'm all ears, Mister Watkinson." Roxanne leaned back and re-arranged her legs to rest her right ankle on her left knee.

Rodney had an eyeful. "Definitely suspenders," he thought. "White undies as well." He was surprised she wore any at all.

He took a sip from his water glass. "I shall proceed then," he said, after clearing his throat. His pulse began to beat a tattoo in his ears as he searched for 'The Relevant Section'.

"Ah! Here it is. 'Female staff shall wear, as in the case of their male counterparts, attire of a sober colour while on duty. The management encourages the wearing of skirts or dresses although these should not be of so bulky a design as to impinge upon the workspace of others... Trouser suits, while frowned upon, are acceptable... Cardigans or sweaters may be worn over a blouse in cooler weather...'

He flipped the page. "'All clothing must be of good quality material, as should footwear.'... Mmmm?.. And it goes on to say, Miss Smith..."

"I'm listening!"

"'Jeans, bare feet, outlandish headgear will not be tolerated.'"

"So, you see, Miss Smith," he summarized, flipping the plasticized sheet over to her side of the desk. "You are out of order and I must ask you to dress appropriately in future."

"Where does it say I am out of order, Mister Watkinson?"

Roxanne uncoiled herself from the chair. She stood with her feet as far apart as her skirt would allow and placed her hands on her hips. Her firm young breasts rose and fell in time with her breathing as she waited for a reply.

"Er?"

"I am not out of order, Mister Watkinson. You are!" Roxanne pointed squarely at his nose. "My blouse is of good quality cotton," she went on reasonably, smoothing the said article of clothing against the curves of her body with her hands. "And white. A sober enough colour, I hope, Mister Watkinson?"

'Mister Watkinson' could only nod.

"My shoes, like my stockings, are black." She stretched a shapely leg and pointed the toe of one shoe. "And of good quality leather." She then proceed to pace towards the office door like a model strutting her stuff on the catwalk. "As is my skirt," she purred over her shoulder. She pivoted round sinuously, then paced back, smoothing her skirt against her thighs and letting her fingertips linger around the hemline.

Rodney could not help but to admire the spectacle with one eye… even though, with his other eye, he was beginning to get pissed off.

Standing once more in front of his desk, feet apart and hands on her hips, Roxanne continued with her little oratory.

"White! Black! Sober colours, Mister Watkinson and of good quality material." Then, moving her hands to the small of her back, she asked, "Would you like to see my underwear?" She made as if to unfasten the waistband of her skirt. "They are white and of good quality cotton."

"That won't be necessary, Miss Smith," Rodney said, getting to his feet hurriedly. He had no doubts that Miss Smith, left to her own devices, would step out of her skirt and parade around, probably tossing her blouse aside for good measure.

Roxanne folded her arms across her breasts and waited while Rodney silently counted to ten. "Sober colours and good quality, yes, Miss Smith. However, the length of you skirt…"

"Is not mentioned in the dress code at all, Mister Watkinson. Not mentioned at all."

Roxanne picked up the plasticized sheet, gave it a slap and tossed it down on the desk. "And I can assure you that my skirt does not impinge upon the workspace of others."

"Your skirt, Miss Smith," Rodney said in exasperation, "barely impinges upon your own work space. That is the problem!" He steadied himself against the desk. Roxanne was a pain in the neck, but the ache she provoked was in his loins. Rodney Watkinson could deny that fact no longer.

The two glared at each other across the desk. It was Roxanne who broke the silence.

"Mister Watkinson," she said. "I am dressed within the guidelines of the bank's dress code and well you know it."

She stood with her arms, once again, folded across her breasts and her weight on one leg.

"Will there be anything else?"

"Not for now, Miss Smith." Rodney wriggled his tie loose. "You may go, but this matter is by no means closed."

Miss Smith spun on her heel and marched out of the office. As she went out the door, she turned and blew Rodney a kiss. She hoped she had not been too hard on him. After all, she didn't want him requesting a transfer.

Once Roxanne had left the office, Rodney retrieved the plasticized sheet. He sat down heavily and scrutinized it.

"What a farce!" he said aloud. He hadn't actually read the thing until this meeting with 'Our Miss Smith'. He flung the sheet into the litter bin in disgust then put his head into his hands. He wondered what to do next. About Roxanne and Gillian.

Our hero had been sitting thus for several minutes, when Mister Snoddlegrass poked his head into the office. "Fancy a cuppa, Rodney?" he said. "You look like you need one and I've just put the kettle on."

Rodney could not help but to laugh. "I'll be along shortly," he said. "Er… Just got a few things to finish off."

"Right then! I'll see you in my office." With that, Mister Snoddlegrass closed the door and went on his way.

Rodney thought that perhaps the old duffer could provide him with some insights. And who could tell? Maybe 'Sammy' even understood women. He got up from behind his desk, straightened his tie out and smoothed his hair back into place.

The meeting with Roxanne may have been a disaster for him, but that was no reason for him to go around looking untidy.

Privately, he agreed with Miss Smith. However, he did have a job to do and resolved to tackle her again at a later date. But this time, he would do his homework first.

Then there was the matter of Gillian, his dream girl. What had got into her? Something that that character 'Le Trevoir' had said flitted through his mind, 'Not unless she fancied a bit o' rough, that is!' Was that it? Rodney began to wonder; was he just a bit of rough to her? Now that she had had what she wanted, was this her way of getting shut of him?

The more his mind ventured along that track, the more convinced he became. A car bonnet was a bit out of the ordinary for that sort of thing. Maybe 'Little Lord Hob-Knob', or whomever, just didn't go in for that. Was that it? Rodney Watkinson, a bit of rough? Pick him up; keep him away from your home, 'I need the exercise… Drop me off at the end of the Manor Drive, please.' Scare him with your driving then take him into the woods. Jump onto your car's bonnet and 'Bob's your Uncle'. Is that how it was?

"Come on, Rodney, lad! Tea's up."

"Coming, Mister Snoddlegrass. I'm on my way."

Had Gillian merely used him? Well, he only had himself to blame if she had. What's more, she could use him again whenever she wanted to as far as he was concerned. The trouble was, he didn't want her to just use him. He had fallen in love with her.

"Roll on Monday," he thought, "Roll on Monday."

≈ ≈ ≈ ≈

Gillian left the Charity Shop a little early that afternoon. The sisters had insisted she go home to bed and, "We'll see you in th' mornin'." They had been of no help, of course. Oh, they had listened to her story; the way they had wanted to hear it, that is.

They had heard how Rodney had been pawing at her all the time that she had been driving. How she had driven faster, just so they would get to a café sooner and she would be able to fend him off for a bit. How he had got her to pull over in Delamere Woods and, with his hand halfway up her skirt, had pretended to star gaze. How he'd got her to take him into a secluded clearing on the pretense of being interested in where she had camped as a school girl. How he had gone on about red skies, sunsets and drunken sailors. How he had got her to strip her sandals and white socks off. 'Getting back to nature' he had called it.

They had heard the outlandish claims he had made on Gillian's behalf. 'More beautiful than a film star that had haunted him, then gone off on a cruise to a sea a long way off'. Or was it? 'Sailed off into the sunset looking beautiful'? Whichever it was, it sounded like a snow job to the experienced ears of the sisters.

They had heard how Rodney had told her that he loved her.

"'e would say that!" Rowena had cut in at that point. "They all say that. I dare say as 'e didn't say owt about love after he had had wot he wanted, did he?"

"Well…"

"Probably rolled over and went to sleep," Rebecca cackled.

Gillian had shaken her head mutely. She had told them that she herself had led him on.

"Don't talk silly, child!" Rebecca snapped. "Men have been doin' that since Adam was a lad. have their way with a girl then make her feel guilty. That's how they work, lass. Take it from one as knows."

"Oh, the scoundrel!" Rowena howled. "To come up 'ere and do this to our Miss Gillian. And 'im walkin' round like Lord Muck, I suppose?"

"Probably proud o' what he's done." Rebecca said. "Thinks he's Cock o' the Walk, no doubt."

"Well, he was strutting a bit, but…"

"We knew it! The rat! Knew it as soon as we set eyes on him we did. Isn't that right, our sis?"

Yes, it was no more that what the sisters had expected since Rodney had first darkened their doorstep. Him and his 'City Ways'. He had given Rowena a funny look as well, the fifth time she had had to measure his inside leg.

"Well, he wouldn't hold still… and then he was leerin' at me."

In summary, the sisters thought that their Miss Gillian must have been easy prey for a city boy like Rodney Watkinson. They had told her that he was a rat, a rodent and the lowest creature that had ever crawled out from under a rock and got up on its hind legs.

He was lower than a snake's belly in a cartwheel rut to have his way with her one day, then send her packing in tears on the next. They would listen to no more excuses on his behalf. He didn't deserve her and that was that. She should forget about him. Rowena herself, however, would still alter the suit. A deal was a deal. If she refused now, that would only serve to bring her down to his level, and Rowena Price was not having that. No way! She may be a bit creative with the fit but, as far as revenge went, that was as far as she would go. Then there was the matter of the fiver.

Once Gillian had left, the shop re-opened for business. Tongues began (as tongues will) to wag. As a result, by the time that she reached the Manor House, Her Ladyship had heard all about it. Jungle Drums, don't you know?

The story that reached Occles-Leigh was well, confusing to say the least. Apparently, Gillian had been seeing a young man by the name of Rodney Rodent. He was a city boy that turned out to be a rat?

Well, Her Ladyship expected that there was a logical explanation behind it all. She was content to wait for her daughter to come home and tell her about it and suspected that it had something to do with the handsome stranger that Gillian had mentioned on Monday morning.

"How was your day, dear?" Her Ladyship called out as Smithers opened the door.

"Thank you, Smithers," Gillian said, stepping inside. "Fine, mother." The sound of TRemor being driven around to the garage was cut off abruptly as the butler closed the door.

"You look a little red around the eyes, dear." Her Ladyship approached and placed a comforting arm around Gillian's shoulders. She attempted to usher her into the Drawing Room.

"I have a headache, mother," Gillian explained, ducking out of her grasp. "I have to lie down for a while." With that, she trotted up the stairs, leaving her mother to look on with a perplexed frown.

Gillian had asked Frank Rutter to give the roadster a thorough wash and wax job. She herself intended to have a good long shower. After that she would lie down, naked between the sheets with curtains drawn and lights off. She had to sort her feelings out. Her feelings for Rodney and herself!

"What is that matter with me?" Gillian thought, getting into bed and pulling the covers over herself. "I wanted to lose my virginity and I succeeded. I wanted to lose it to Rodney Blue-Eyes and again, success. I wanted to act out a little fantasy of mine involving the car bonnet and again, nothing but success. I wanted to try being a bit less sensible and I certainly succeeded there. So, why do I feel so bad about it all? Rodney told me that he loved me. Do 'they' really all say that? Does Rodney really love me? Could he, or any other man come to that, really love a girl that would perform like that? On a car bonnet in the woods? With someone she had only known for three days? Do I really love you, my Rodney? Have I told you that I do? I do!"

She hoped that by Monday she would have her feelings sorted out and be able to face her... her... her lover, as she realized he had now become. Meanwhile, she wondered what those twits at the Charity Shop would spread around. Them and their twisted version of events.

"Oh, drat those sisters!" she sobbed. "Why didn't I keep my mouth shut? Why didn't I stay sensible? Sensible and chaste! Life was much simpler then."

Before falling into a troubled sleep a thought entered her head, "Could this be what Mrs. Morgan foresaw in the tea leaves on Tuesday morning?"

The Heiress and the Banker
Chapter Nine
Those Monday Morning Blues

We re-join the story on Rodney's second Monday in Middlewich and find that busy young man seated behind his desk. He is bent over his books, perspiration drips from his forehead. His jacket, draped over the back of his chair, had been there for hours. His shirt sleeves are pushed up above his elbows. Just recently, Rodney had yanked his tie off and snatched his shirt collar open.

"Damned paperwork!" he growled. "Should tell them to shove it."

The office was stifling. It was already half-past-eleven and he was way behind in his work. Rodney had the helm, Samuel being away on 'Business'; making a long weekend out of a short one. He had given Rodney Friday off and now, apparently, it was his turn.

"Could at least have given me some warning," Rodney muttered. "Get here to a note. 'Ship's all yours, Rodney, lad. I'll be back in the morning. Don't go running 'er aground. Samuel.' Must think he's Captain Bligh." He had had to help himself to breakfast as well. Brunhilde was away. A weekend at the seaside with a friend. The publican looking after the hotel in her absence did not 'Muck about making breakfasts for somebody else's guests, my lad!'

Then there was the matter of Gillian. "Gillian, Gillian, Gillian." He had not been able to get hold of her all weekend, although he had certainly tried. He could not get her off his mind.

The weekend had been uneventful, at least in comparison with his adventures in the 'Boring North'.

He had spent the time in London as he had intended; tying up loose ends, riding his motorbike and making sure that his mum was all right.

Of course, his mother had insisted on feeding him up. As if he needed it on top of Brunhilde Braithewaite's cooking. Apart from those activities, our hero had bent his elbow a time or two down the pub with his mates… and phoned Gillian. To no avail! If he managed to get past the butler, a task in itself, he only succeeded in getting the Colonel on the line. Then he would get short shrift. Wasn't even allowed to introduce himself properly before the line went dead. An ominous silence! A damned nuisance. So, as pleasant as his weekend in London had been, Rodney had been anxious to get back to Middlewich and his one true love. Back to Miss Gillian Brereton-Holbeck and her TR5. He hoped that by now she had gotten over her moodiness. He would soon know. He was to meet her at 'Rhodas' at mid-day.

Rodney glanced at his watch, then swept the stack of papers off his desk. He crossed his arms, one over the other on the desk top, then lay his head against them. He let out a long sigh.

A tap on the door was quickly followed by Roxanne Smith entering his office. She was carrying two mugs of tea. Rodney quickly sat up.

"This is a first, Miss Smith," he said, tucking his shirt more firmly into his waistband.

Roxanne walked, in her seductive manner, towards him. She was surprised at his untidy appearance. He had been his usual smart self the last time she had been in the office.

"What's the to-do, Miss Smith?" Rodney said, surprised. "Bringing me tea?"

Roxanne set the mugs down on the polished top of the desk.

"I've heard Old Mister Snoddlegrass say that you like it hot and sweet, Mister Watkinson," she breathed. Her blouse was open by the 'regulation' three buttons. "I hope this is hot enough," she added, crossing one leg over the other as she sat down.

Rodney noticed that his assistant was wearing black undies today and, as her skirt rode up her thighs, his breath caught. He was jolted by the realization that he had actually missed the little trollop.

"Please take a seat, Miss Smith," he said.

"Thank you, Mister Watkinson," Roxanne purred, making herself more comfortable. "I will." She ran a forefinger over her pouting lips, closed her hand into a fist and rested her chin on her knuckles. Roxanne looked longingly into Rodney's eyes, brown eyes peering from under long lashes. The object of her adoration reached self-consciously for a mug of tea. He wavered between the two.

"They are both hot and sweet, Mister Watkinson, if that is what is bothering you," Roxanne said helpfully. She pulled the hem of her skirt back a little further. "I hope they are to your taste." She smiled sweetly, undoing another blouse button; thus revealing a nicely filled lace bra.

Rodney was impressed. However, he had enough on his mind already and didn't need further frustrations at Miss Smith's hands.

"Very nice, Roxanne," he began firmly. "But this has gone far enough. Too far, in fact." He made an effort to keep his eyes on Roxanne's. "You're a trainee bank clerk, Miss Smith, not a striptease artist. Please! Button yourself up, sit in a more ladylike fashion and tell me what is on your mind. You didn't bring me tea at this time of day without reason, I'm sure."

Roxanne was taken aback; but also quite pleased. Mister Watkinson had noticed her at last and… he was so masterful when he wanted to be.

"Ohhh! Mister Watkinson!" she gasped, looking down at her blouse. "What must you think?" Quickly buttoning herself up.

"How my blouse buttons came undone, I have no idea." Sitting up straight, uncrossing her legs then pulling her skirt primly into place. "They're always doing that."

Roxanne Smith felt jubilant. The man of her dreams had noticed her at last and, on top of that, had called her by her first name.

"That's better," Rodney said briskly. "Now, what is on your mind, Miss Smith?" He took a sip from the mug of tea he had chosen while waiting for Roxanne's reply.

"What do you think of it?" she asked, indicating the tea with a nod of her head while, at the same time, running her hands over her midriff. She looked up alluringly at her boss and smoothed her skirt over her thighs.

"A little tart," he replied, taking another sip of the tea. "A little…" he clicked his tongue thoughtfully. "A little tart." He took another swallow of the tea. "I could get used to it though."

"Mmm!" Miss Smith 'Mmm'd' thoughtfully, thinking over what her supervisor had just said. "Mmm!"

"Now, Miss Smith. The reason for your visit?" Rodney could see he had Roxanne off balance. He placed his tea mug down firmly. It was good to get the upper hand for a change.

"Well, Mister Watkinson, it's like this." (Did he call me a little tart or the tea?) "It's personal and not really my business but…" Roxanne took a swallow of her tea. "You deserve to know the truth." She was relieved to find that the tea was not tart at all.

"Go on, Miss Smith. Time is ticking and I have an appointment to keep."

"It's not easy and I don't like being a snitch, Mister Watkinson, but I'm the only one that is likely to tell you. All Middlewich knows by now anyway."

"Please get to the point, Roxanne." Rodney glanced at his watch in irritation.

Miss Smith took a giddy breath. First name again. She took another gulp of tea in an effort to steel herself. What she had to tell Rodney would be no easy task.

"It's about that 'ussy... er... Miss Brereton-Holbeck. The young woman you 'ave been seein'... I know you've been seein' 'er... and that." She paused, then blurted, "She's engaged."

"She's what?"

"She got engaged. You know? To be married?" Roxanne replied, wagging her third finger left hand under Rodney's nose. "It 'appened while you were away at th' weekend," she added in a sad voice, letting her eyes drop away. She didn't like the hurt expression that had crept into her boss's eyes.

"What? That's preposterous, Roxanne," our hero spluttered. "What are you talking about?"

Miss Smith gulped down more tea, then placed the mug on the floor by her feet. She began her tale, this time in earnest.

"Last Satdee nate," she stated, slipping, in her unease, into the dialect she used away from the bank. "Me an' me sister, Andrea were at th' 'Cool Cat's Nate Club in Nantwich. We was on th' balcony in th' Sweethearts' lounge eyein' up... well... we was on th' balcony and in walks that 'ussy... your girlfriend... wi' a bloke. A right toffee-nosed get an all be th' looks o' 'im."

Roxanne reached for her tea, drained the mug, then set it back down on the floor. She started to fiddle nervously with her blouse buttons.

Rodney did not look happy. "I'm listening, Miss Smith," he said in a stuffy tone. "Please continue."

"Well, they walks over to one of th' little booths, you know, them as are used for smoochin' an' such like?" Rodney nodded. "Then they sits down on opposite sides o' th' little table. She looks 'appy, smug, a great smile plastered across 'er chops. Then 'e gets summat out o' 'is pocket. Summat as makes 'er eyes pop near out o' 'er 'ead. 'e puts this summat on th' table and th' next thing as me an' me sister knows, 'e's down on one knee. It looked like 'e was proposin' an' th' 'ussy just sat there an' let 'im put th' ring, which is what th' summat turned out to be, on 'er finger..."

Roxanne pressed herself back into her seat as Rodney sprang to his feet, sending his chair flying into the wall behind.

"Roxanne! Please!" He ran his fingers through his hair and massaged his scalp. "You are talking about the girl I love. She is not a hussy. I cannot believe this cock and bull story. Just what is your game?" He leaned over the desk and glared at the girl on the other side.

"It's not a game, Mister Watkinson. It's true!" Roxanne said defiantly. "If you'd o' seen 'ow chuffed your girlfriend was, examining that ring while th' toffee-nosed get was still down on one knee like a big pillock, maybe you'd see a bit o' sense."

Roxanne was near to tears, her blouse buttons all undone. "She never did deserve you, Rodney. There, I've called you by your first name. Oh, can't you see, love? She's a two-timin' 'ussy. She used you and I 'ate 'er." The distraught young woman burst into tears.

Rodney did not know what to make of this performance. Miss Smith looked wretched; blouse all undone, skirt rucked up above her stocking tops and now crying into her hands. He had to do something. He stepped around the desk, pushing the discarded paperwork aside with a sweep of his foot, and offered her some tissues from a box on his desk.

"Come on now, Roxanne," he said. "Pull yourself together. I'm sure we'll find there is a reasonable explanation for all this. Here, please. Dry your eyes."

Miss Smith dabbed her eyes then blew her nose loudly.

"I doubt that it was Gillian you saw anyway," Rodney said in an offhand manner. A manner that he did not actually feel. The story bore out his own inner feelings about being used. A glance at his watch revealed that he would know the rights of things soon. He decided that if he saw a ring on Gillian's finger he would walk straight past her, ignore her, and that way at least salvage some of his pride. The decision was made and discarded in the blink of an eye. He knew he could never ignore Gillian, no matter what.

Roxanne managed to get control of her emotions long enough to speak. "Rodney, 'ow can you be so blind?" she cried, jumping to her feet and sending the tea mug careening across the room, her chair with it.

"'I doubt that it was Gillian you saw anyway'," she mimicked, sniffing back the tears. "'Do you 'ave a sports car, Miss Prim?'" she went on, in the same mocking tone. "'I 'ave a TR5 actuwawly!'" in a haughty voice then, demandingly, "What is it about 'er? She's a two-timin', cheatin', man grabbin' 'ussy. I love you, I do… and stop lookin' at your watch!" Roxanne yelled, pummeling his chest with her balled fists. "Why are men so stupid-stupid-stupid?"

Miss Smith collapsed into her flabbergasted supervisor's arms and sobbed violently into his shirt. She wrapped her arms tightly around him taking deep ragged breaths, absolutely inconsolable in her grief.

"Come on now, Roxanne. Get a grip of yourself, girl!" Rodney said sternly. He looked at his watch again, this time over the top of the weeping girl's head. "I don't know what to say. I'm sorry that you love me, I can't help that. You'll get over me, if that's any consolation. If I'd have met you first, things might have been different. Who knows…?"

That was it! Miss Smith, tears suddenly dry, pushed herself away from her unfeeling idol.

"You did meet me first, Rodney Watkinson!" she yelled, buttoning up her blouse and looking at him accusingly. "You did," wagging a finger into the poor man's face. "Then she came along, waving a twenty pound note under your nose. 'I'd like some small change for this, Mister.' Small change? That's more than I make in a week, Rodney Watkinson, more than I make in a week. Well, if it's money that turns you on, 'ow can a girl like me even 'ope to compete?"

She straightened out her clothing and stamped out of the office, turning at the door to yell, "Well, you've 'ad your chance with me, Rodney Watkinson. Don't come runnin' back when Miss Rich Britches, the 'ussy, as done with you." She burst into tears again. "Because I won't be interested. You see if I'm not." Then she was gone… heading straight for the 'Ladies'.

The Head Teller, Mrs. Davies, was right on her heels.

"What the bloody 'ell have I done now?" our hero muttered. He gathered the office chairs and tea mugs up. The paperwork almost went into the litter bin, but he thought better of it. He shoved it in a heap on his desk to be dealt with after lunch. Hopefully by then, he and his assistant would be in better frames of mind.

≈ ≈ ≈ ≈ ≈

Shortly afterwards, our hero found himself pacing up and down in agitation outside 'Rhodas'.

The townsfolks were giving him curious looks as they stepped off the narrow pavement to avoid colliding with him.

"Where is she?"

There had been no sign of his one true love when he had arrived at the bakery and the church clock had already been chiming the quarter-past-the-hour as he had trotted up Wheelock Street. Rodney had looked into the bakery's big front window when he first got there… no sign of her inside either.

He gave up pacing and stood with his back to the window, looking up and down the busy street then staring in the direction of the Charity Shop willing Gillian to appear.

"Is it Rodney, ducks?"

He turned to find himself confronted by the matronly features of Big Rhoda. "That's right, yes," he answered. "Can I help you, Rhoda?"

"I think you'd better come inside for a cup o' tea, ducks. There's a letter for you… from young Miss Gillian. She was upset. I'd o' come out sooner, but you know 'ow it is at dinner time?"

Rodney, bemused, followed Rhoda into the bakery. The customers avoided his eye as, to the sound of mutterings and whispers, she led him into the kitchen.

"You sit yourself over there, ducks," she said, waving a hand towards a cluttered table in the corner. She took an envelope from her apron pocket and handed it to him. "I won't be a minute."

Rodney went to the table and pulled out a chair. He had the envelope ripped open before he was even sat down.

To My Darling Blue-My Eyes,'

'I'm sorry I couldn't meet you today, I really am. I don't really expect you to show up anyway but maybe, someday, you'll have lunch with that Jezebel you so admire at the bank. She is better for you anyway. At least she knows what she is and you know what you will be getting. Not like with me.

As for us, we started out so well and then I messed things up. This whole mess is entirely my fault, I see that now and you mustn't go blaming yourself. Even if you are what they say you are... You may even believe that you love me, but I am no good for you, I know that now.

My life has gone crazy, I don't know what I want anymore. Last Wednesday night I behaved like a woman for the first time in my life, or thought I was doing at the time. Now I am engaged to another, sort of. Oh, Rodney, can you ever forgive me? I have to go away and find myself, I am under so much pressure here. You have no idea! I can't explain it all, I just know that I have to get away.

Goodbye and Good Luck to you and that Jezebel.

I'll always love you!

Yours Forever,

Your Mixed Up Strumpet,

Gillian xxx

Rodney had lowered himself into the seat while reading the letter. Now he sat back, turning it over in his hands. On the back there was a postscript.

P.S. I'll leave this with the Rhodas for when you two show up there. Look after her and remind her to wipe the cream off her mouth.

He tossed the letter down on the table in front of him. Some of the ink had run. "She must have been crying," he thought absently.

"There y'are, ducks. Get that down you. I've made it a bit stronger than what we serve up front." Rhoda, having returned from giving him a minute, placed a steaming hot cup of black tea in front of him. "You'll feel better for it," she said. "The path of true love never did run smooth." Rodney felt Rhoda's big hand on his shoulder. "Tea's on th' house. I expect you'll get over 'er... in time." Big Rhoda turned and walked away, unable to stand by and see such a nice young man as Rodney on the verge of tears.

≈ ≈ ≈ ≈ ≈

Meanwhile, Rodney's 'One True Love' and 'Mixed Up Strumpet' was, at this time, haring, full throttle, down the Motorway. Birmingham and Spaghetti Junction were already far behind. She had her passport in her pocket, a suitcase in her car... and an ache in her heart. She had told no-one of her plans, other than to leave a note for her mother; that, and the letter for Rodney, was all. Neither communication stated her destination. Our heroine had to find herself. She thought that Monte-Carlo, with all its night life, would be a good place to start looking. First though, she had some business to take care of... In Switzerland.

The Heiress and the Banker
Chapter Ten
Betrothal

Our heroine bore along, heart torn asunder, thinking over the events of the previous week. Meeting Rodney Blue-Eyes; their whirlwind romance; last Wednesday night in the woods; Thursday and Rodney's cruel remarks. The ecstasy and the heartbreak of the most wonderful week of her young life.

Gillian knew that she and Rodney would have got over their lovers' tiff; if he had not gone down to London at such a critical time; if she had not compounded her first mistake (the car bonnet in the woods) by making a bigger one in Rodney's absence.

If! Such a small word, yet it had changed her life irrevocably. Saturday night! If she could change just one series of events in her life, it would be those of last Saturday night.

Our heroine had, of course, gone dancing with Cedric. She was much too decent to put her old friend off, boring as his company could be at times. Besides, she had felt that a night out dancing with such a reliable fellow might buck her up a bit. She remembered waking up early on Friday morning to the sound of drizzling rain. As she had looked out the window, one of the dogs had slunk across the courtyard; head down and miserable in the damp. She had spent most of that day in bed. Yes, she'd needed cheering up a bit and, at the time, the night out with Cedric had done the job.

After a nice dinner at the Manor House, the pair had set off for the 'Cool Cat's Night Club' in Cedric's Jaguar. Gillian had listened to some classical music on the radio while her friend had recounted the story of the Master of the Hunt and the courting couple.

"Turned out that everyone had seen them…" This in itself had served to cheer her up as she knew exactly when to laugh, when to make a comment and just what to say… all without paying the slightest bit of attention. However, Gillian was in for a bit of a surprise once they reached the night club.

"Gillian, my love! You look divine," Cedric had said. He had held the door for her as she had stepped out of the car.

"Why, thank you, Cedric," she had replied. At the time, Gillian had thought he was just practicing some love lines for a girl he had met at the hunt. She wouldn't have put it past him.

Once inside the night club, they had had a couple of drinks and chatted for a while. 'Cool Cat's wasn't exclusive, but the management did encourage a certain standard of dress. This meant that, suit and tie being a pre-requisite for gentlemen, Cedric Ponsomby-Smythe did not look out of place. Gillian, on the other hand, always looked out of place. She stood out wherever she went. That night she had worn her figure hugging blue dress, the skirt of which was flared. This, and the shoes she wore that night, was her favourite dancing outfit. She had worn her hair brushed out and loose.

After dancing the light fantastic, Cedric had suggested that they take a break. It was then that he had led her into the 'Sweethearts' Lounge'. The Siren Sisters happened to be on the balcony. They were, as we have heard, eyeing up the talent. 'Miss Rich Britches, the 'ussy' and her 'Toffee-nosed-get-of-a-boyfriend' were spotted as they entered.

"I must say, you are a superb dancer, Gillian, my love!" Cedric remarked. The bold gallant had got a couple of drinks in and placed one in her hand. Once more, Gillian found herself being led, this time to one of the booths; 'Them as are used for smoochin' an' such.'

"If I'd have only known, I could have stopped it then," Gillian thought, still in the fast lane; still going fast. It looked like it might rain soon, the sky was darkening to the south. Our heroine continued to punish herself; going over that which she could not change.

"This suit you," Cedric had asked, indicating one of the cosey booths.

"Suits me," Gillian replied. She slid into the seat, Cedric sat opposite. He had looked uncomfortable, fiddling with the drink he had placed on the small table between them. "Are you all right, Cedric?" she said. "You look a little nervous. Scared of me?"

"Perhaps a little," he muttered then, out loud. "You look absolutely divine, Gillian. Absolutely divine. That blue dress always has brought out the best in you."

"What? This old thing?" She looked divine? Again?

Our heroine had started to think that the needle had stuck when her old friend, her 'cousin', cleared his throat and blurted, "Look here, old love, this isn't easy for me. More used to four-legged foxes you know? But... well... I have a proposition to make and..." He pulled a little velvet covered box from his pocket. Green! "I have something for you."

Gillian remembered her astonishment as Cedric had placed the box on the table top to open the hinged lid.

"But, Cedric...?" she had gasped.

She had not been able to take her eyes from that which they beheld. The most beautiful diamond ring that she had ever seen reclined majestically on a tiny velvet cushion.

"It's beautiful!" she murmured.

She remembered half hearing Cedric speak. "It is my dearest hope, my darling, that you will accept this humble token of my esteem." He had offered the ring, it now lay in the palm of his hand, as he had continued. "Gillian, light of my life, darling of mine, I have always been yours."

She had not been able to help herself. Gillian had plucked the 'Humble Token' of Cedric's esteem out of his hand. She had had to have a closer look. "But what…?"

"Oh, Gillian, my darling. This may seem a little sudden to you," Cedric said as he stood up and moved to her side. "But don't you see? We were made for each other. We are a perfect match."

Gillian knew, in hindsight of course, that she should have given the ring back right then. She should have told her old friend that she knew what he was about to propose; she should have told him not to. She should have told him that she loved him… like a cousin, like the dear old friend (tiresome though he could be) that he had always been. She should have told him anything, as long as it had been a bit more coherent than, "But what…?" all the while examining the ring as she gripped it firmly between finger and thumb.

She had finally torn her eyes away from the mesmeric jewel. She remembered the determined look on Cedric's face. He had got down on one knee, first placing his milk white handkerchief on the floor. All he had lacked was a sword at his side and a hat (complete with feather) with which to sweep the rug.

"Oh, Gillian," he said. "That diamond pales in the light from your eyes, darling. Yet still, I ask you, accept it and with it my humble offer of marriage."

Our heroine's mouth had dropped open, but Cedric had not finished yet.

"You are my inspiration, the force that makes my life complete. Every time I see you, it is like turning a corner on some lonely stretch of road to be confronted by a snow-capped mountain, sunlight glancing off its lofty peak, and I feel truly alive."

Gillian had been (and still was) dumfounded by this speech. She thought it more beautiful than the ring itself.

His somewhat melodramatic proposal of marriage over, Cedric had taken the ring from Gillian's unresisting grasp. She had followed his movements with her eyes to see him slip the bauble onto her third finger left hand. Cedric, still on one knee, looked questioningly at his darling.

"Cedric, what can I say?" Gillian asked. She pulled her hand away from his and studied the ring anew. She smiled. (The Siren Sisters had seen enough.) Cedric had made her feel wonderful, but she could not marry him.

"Yes?" Cedric suggested hopefully.

"Oh, Cedric, what else could a girl say to an offer like that but yes…?" She had meant to go on and say, "But you and I have been brought up too closely together for me to consider you as a beau."

She would have declined his offer graciously had not Cedric, on hearing the word he had longed to hear, jumped to his feet and cried, "Darling! You have made me the happiest man on Earth. We can set the day at your leisure. A long courtship if you like. I've waited all my life, I can wait until next Spring. I've no objections to that…"

Gillian had looked on in puzzlement. She had said yes?

"…if that is what you want, my love. But come. We have tarried over long. Her Ladyship has arranged a little reception for us at the Manor House. Nothing special, a few friends and family. My father is likely thrashing the Colonel at billiards as we speak."

"Reception? Billiards?" Gillian should have asserted herself and put a stop to it all. She had wanted to, but then… everything had been arranged. She couldn't see getting a better offer that this either, not now. Not after last Wednesday night. Rodney Blue-Eyes had been a flash in the pan, he had treated her cruelly. But… "Do you love me, Cedric?"

Cedric had taken both her hands in his, kissed each in turn, then looked deep into her eyes. "We were made for each other, my love."

"But do you…?"

"Before tonight, I was too afraid, or shy perhaps, to mention anything to you along that line. That's why I was always going on about foxes and hounds and generally making a fool of myself." He had let go of Gillian's hands and placed an encouraging arm around her shoulders. "Let us make haste, my love," he said. "We have an announcement to make."

"It sounds to me like you have been making announcements already, Cedric."

"Well, I did mention that I might…"

It still hadn't felt quite right to Gillian, however, her old friend had surprised her; she'd known him all her life and tonight had discovered that she didn't know him at all. His proposal had been so romantic… Had he said he loved her?

After her silly-school-girl behaviour of Wednesday night, she had decided to make an adult decision. She wanted to be treated like an adult; she would start behaving like one. "You're right, Cedric," she said. And after this came to fruition there would be no more 'Miss Gillian'. "We do have an announcement to make."

She reached over and picked up the velvet covered box. She had had a 'Day in the Bar'; now it was time to return to the 'Snug' side of life. The life she knew best. The cut and thrust of life amongst the working class was not for her after all. "And I will marry you next Spring. I will learn to love you. But do you…?"

"No time to waste, my beloved," Cedric said. "We have to get on."

After that it had just been a matter of relaxing; of going with the flow. Our heroine had been swept away; borne along on the riptide of events that followed her decision to say yes.

However, by the time that Sunday night had come around, Gillian had been filled with doubt. Marriage was a life-time commitment, or ought to be. She did not want to let Cedric down; she did not want to let herself down. Rodney had been a flash-in-the-pan, that was all over… but…

Gillian had sought out her mother. "I have to talk to you alone," she had whispered after her betrothed and his father had left. They had shared a room in the west wing of the Manor House over the weekend. "I'll meet you in my room, shall I?"

Her Ladyship had merely nodded, the Colonel being ensconced (sleepy eyed) in his best easy chair. "Another snifter of brandy would be just the job, Sir William," he muttered, then drifted off to sleep again.

Sitting on the edge of the bed, Her Ladyship had listened patiently while her daughter told all about her brief affair with the blue-eyed stranger. The same blue-eyed stranger she had first heard mentioned only six short days before. The story she heard was basically the same as the rumours going around, but with a different slant. Somehow, each illogical step seemed to lead logically to the next. Her Ladyship thought, privately, that in Gillian's shoes she probably would have behaved in a similar fashion, but that she herself would have enjoyed it more.

"Where did you say that clearing was, Gillian?"

"Mother! Please! This is serious."

"Sorry, go on."

After telling the full story of Rodney of the Blue-Eyes and her mixed up feelings for him, Gillian had gone on to tell of what a romantic and thoughtful chap Cedric had turned out to be. Of how he had swept her off her feet with his proposal of marriage, the last thing she had expected from him (or anyone else for that matter). Of how he had presented her with the ring that everyone had been admiring all weekend. Of how he had told her that he considered it a humble token of his esteem, a mere bauble and that it paled in the light of her eyes. Of how, in her determination to give that Rodney one in the eye, she had asked her new fiancé to pull over on the way back from Nantwich the previous evening. Of how they had made love on the back seat of the Jaguar. Of how she had thought that it had been proper. They were as good as married anyway.

Gillian told her mother of how her feelings for Cedric had changed; she no longer thought of him as a cousin. She told her mother of how she could not forget Rodney and of how she felt like she had become a scarlet woman. She told her mother that she didn't know what to do, even as the tears began to well up behind her eyes.

Her Ladyship had known that this was coming and that it was no time for sentiment.

"You have to learn to stand on your own two feet, Gillian," she said. "To make decisions and stand by them, hard as it may be."

Gillian remembered the severe way her mother had looked at her. "Do you love this Rodney fellow?" she asked.

"Yes… I think I do… but…"

"No 'buts', yes is your answer. Now, how about Cedric? Do you love him?"

"Yes… I think I do… but…"

"No 'buts', Gillian. You love them both? Is that what you are trying to tell your mother? That you love them both?"

"In different ways, yes. But what am I to do?"

"Only you can answer that, Gillian. You know your own feelings better than anyone else and I can't make your decisions for you anymore. It would not help you at all if I did. I can offer you this though, an engagement ring and a bit of fun in the back seat of a car is not final. Neither is love on a car bonnet, else where would any of us be? You're a big girl, Gillian, a grown woman."

At this point, Her Ladyship had stood up. "I'll see you in the morning. Things generally look different after a good night's sleep. Goodnight, dear." With that, Her Ladyship had pecked her daughter on the cheek and left the room.

Gillian had watched her mother walk away. It was time for another crying do… and there's nothing wrong with that. Emotions were meant to be shown, else why do we have them? Shortly afterwards, she fell into a deep and dreamless sleep, free of emotional turmoil for a brief eternity.

Bright and early on the Monday morning, our heroine was up and about, decision made. She left a note for her mother:- 'Please look after Redfers and Blackie. I have to find myself and make some sense out of things. Tell Cedric not to worry. He can have his ring back, but it won't come off… etc. etc.'

After that she had written the breathless letter that Big Rhoda had handed to Rodney later that same day. She had then got on with the business of getting underway.

She had lowered her suitcase out the window on tied together bed sheets; walked nonchalantly along the gallery landing, crept down the staircase and out through the back door. Then she had brought her roadster around as quietly as possible, her foot a mere feather on the throttle pedal, picked up her suitcase from the courtyard and was on her way. Only the dogs had observed her leaving. No-one had waved her goodbye; not even the bed sheets. They had just hung there, limp in the still morning air, from her bedroom window.

Now she was driving relentlessly south, into a storm. The sky overhead turning black as she pursued her fate. A fate already written in the tea-leaves at the bottom of a cup? A fate that Mefanway Morgan had seen? Seen and not breathed a word about?

The Heiress and the Banker
Chapter Eleven
After the Ball is Over

Rodney stuffed the letter into his trouser pocket as he left the bakery. He hadn't drunk any of the tea; he hadn't been able to. He felt as if his worst nightmare had come true. He'd met the girl of his dreams; she'd loved and left him. That is, if she had really loved him in the first place.

'I'll always love you!' the note said.

"Then why has she left?" he ground out.

Hands stuffed into his pockets, shoulders hunched, Rodney stepped back into the street. An old man, still wearing a winter overcoat, cleared his throat noisily and spat. His phlegm landed right at Rodney's feet. He gave the ancient a dirty look, but the old man just carried on his way.

"What a place!" Rodney muttered unhappily.

Now that he'd lost Gillian he wondered what he had ever seen in Middlewich in the first place. It had lost the rosy glow it had seemed to possess the week before. He now saw it as the dull grey working class town it had first appeared to be.

"Go on, spit on the street, you old bugger. What does it matter now?"

Without his rose coloured glasses; without his heroine; our hero could not be bothered to be bothered. Still, he was here and here he would stay. Gillian may yet return and, if not, "Just have to make the best of it. I'll get over her. I should be used to that by now."

Gillian had said that she would always love him, but what good was that when she had already left?

"Mind out, lad!"

"Sorry!" Rodney shook himself from his musings. Bumping into passers-by wouldn't help. He started to wonder about the 'Toffee-Nosed-Get' that Gillian was apparently betrothed to.

Where did he fit into all this? Was he away with her even now? Helping her to 'Find Herself'? Or was that all a load of nonsense meant to put him off?

No, that sounded far too elaborate. Putting him off would have taken a simple 'Thank you, but no thank you!' He decided that the other bloke was probably as bad off as himself.

"Highly strung. I should have known that a goddess would be highly strung."

≈ ≈ ≈ ≈ ≈

Cedric Ponsomby-Smythe was beside himself. "Left?" he spluttered. "Left? What the dickens are you talking about, Smithers? Left?"

The butler stood four square in the doorway of the Manor House. "The staff have been informed that Miss Gillian has gone away on an extended sabbatical, Sir. We are not to speak of her around the Colonel, nor are we to speculate or form opinions. I'm sorry, Sir, but that is all I can tell you. Good day, Sir." Smithers attempted to close the door, but found himself shoving against Cedric's lean hunt-hardened frame.

"How dare you, Smithers? I'm part of the family. Just what is going on? The young lady of the house and I are to be wed, and well you know it." Cedric gave an extra push. "Stand aside, Sir, I say!"

Now Smithers had been a butler long enough to know when it was time to withdraw. He stood back and adopted a respectful stance.

The young Ponsomby-Smythe entered the front hall with a flourish, handing the butler his driving gloves and hat. "That's better, Smithers. What on Earth has got into you anyway?" He stepped closer and sniffed. "Not been at the brandy bottle again have you?" Cedric folded his arms across his chest and held the butler's eye. "Well? Speak up, man."

"If the young sir would permit…"

"Oh, stop being so pompous, Harold!" Her Ladyship strode into the front hall. "Cedric? Join me in the sitting room, please." She held out an inviting hand, a look of sympathy on her face.

"Thank you," Cedric said, going over to join her. He gave the butler a look. "I'm glad to see that someone in this house still knows the meaning of courtesy."

"We'll take coffee in the sitting room, when you have finished gaping, Smithers."

The butler pulled himself together. It was not a very good day. First Miss Gillian doing a runner, then being called 'Sir' by that young upstart and now, worst of all, Her Ladyship addressing him as Harold. He went about his business with a shake of his head. Not a very good day at all.

≈ ≈ ≈ ≈ ≈

Goddess or not, our hero had more immediate matters to deal with. A change of shirt being the first on his list. He had to go back to the 'Occles-Leigh Arms'. Thanks to the Jezebel he apparently admired so much at the bank, the one he wore was streaked with mascara and salty tear stains.

Then he would have to counsel that same Jezebel again. Quite apart from Rodney's grief over the treatment dealt him by his dream girl; quite apart from Miss Smith's School-Girl-Crush; life at Avonlea's Bank, Middlewich had to go on. And Rodney

Watkinson had the helm, at least until Mister Snoddlegrass got back.

"Must be away with Brunhilde," Rodney muttered. He crossed the street to the car park behind the 'White Boar'.

Rodney pulled his shoulders back, lifted his chin and lengthened his stride. He had plenty of work to do. He would immerse himself in it. He would try to follow the advice he had given so easily to Roxanne Smith. He would pull himself together; get a grip of himself. Above all, he would try to forget Miss Gillian Brereton-Holbeck and her TR5. Even if she did come back, she would still not be his. During the course of a rather lazy afternoon, our hero came up with a plan of action. It was a rather hazy one but, any plan is better than none, as they say.

Thanks to Mrs. Davies, the problem of Roxanne Smith had been solved, albeit temporarily. Rodney had had to offer his apologies for the cruel way he had treated her that morning, stress being the only excuse he could come up with for his inexcusable behaviour. Miss Smith had accepted this and had stated the she herself had been under some stress of late and maybe they could just start over again on a better footing? Rodney had agreed; Mrs. Davies had been relieved; and Roxanne tickled Rodney's palm when they sealed the deal with a handshake.

As the two ladies were leaving the office, the Head Teller held back. "She'll be wearing trouser suits after this, Mister Watkinson. Maybe then I'll get a bit more work out of them two out front there."

"Thank you, Mrs. Davies. I appreciate your assistance in this matter."

"Any time, Mister Watkinson, any time. I know she makes it difficult for you young men. Old Mister Snoddlegrass isn't entirely immune from her wiles either." She gave a quick nod of her head. "Well, must get on."

Miss Smith had been making it difficult for him all right, but that didn't change matters. Gillian had done a runner and he loved her. What to do? He would go to the source of the problem. He would pay a visit to the Manor House, talk to Gillian's parents. He would find out where the 'Toffee-Nosed-Get' fit into the scheme of things and find out where he himself stood. Obviously not very high in the Colonel's opinion. The Colonel wouldn't give him the time of day on the phone, which meant he would have to show up uninvited. And he would, but not in jeans and leather jacket. Nor his business suit for that matter. No, he would wear his new Saville Row suit. It should be ready. "Five pounds and you can pick it up next Monday…" he remembered Rowena saying. So, that then, was our hero's plan. A bold one it was too, under the circumstances.

$$\approx \approx \approx \approx \approx$$

Later that afternoon, Rodney strode into the Charity Shop. It seemed empty without his dream girl.

"Hello!" Rodney said pleasantly.

"Well, look what the foul wind's blown in, our Rowena."

"Cat dragged it in, more like." Rowena emerged from the passageway. "Just look at it. Bloody cheek, I call it." She went over to the clothes rack. "'ere's your suit! I'm surprised you've got the brass neck to come in 'ere after what you did to our Miss Gillian I am."

"Yes, you brass-necked bugger!" Rebecca added, wagging a finger into Rodney's face.

"But, ladies, I…?"

"They all say that. But a deal is a deal. 'ere's your suit!" Rowena repeated. She looked him in the eye. "Five pounds for the suit… and five pounds for me trouble." She held out the suit with one hand, the other open and, it appeared to Rodney, claw-like and grasping.

Rodney pulled out his wallet, counted out a fiver and five ones and handed the money over. "Thank you, Rowena, I…"

"It's Mrs. Price to you, young man!" she screeched, snatching the money from his hand.

"And Mrs. Smallwood," her sister added, in much the same tone.

"Thank you, Mrs. Price." Rodney took the suit. "Mrs. Smallwood. Good day!" He hurried out of there, hoping he would get a better reception at the Manor House.

"Brass-necked bugger!" he heard as the door clicked shut behind him.

≈ ≈ ≈ ≈ ≈

Later that evening, a knock on the open door of the billiard room preceded an announcement from the butler.

The Colonel looked up from his solo game. "Who did you say, Smithers?" He would learn to beat Sir William yet.

"A Mister Watkinson," the butler repeated. "A young man. Something to do with the matter of Miss Gillian, Sir." His face, thanks to long practice over the years, revealed nothing.

But the Colonel knew who the young man waiting at the door was. "I see! Well, don't leave him standing there, man."

He turned back to his game, cast a steely glare along the length of his cue and snapped, "Send him off! Before I set the dogs on him."

"As you wish, Sir."

The butler turned away and, although deporting himself in his usual stately manner, narrowly missed colliding with Her Ladyship.

"We'll see the young man in the drawing room, Smithers," she countermanded. "Please show him in." She stood back from the doorway to allow the butler to pass. "Cuthbert?"

A ball ricocheted smartly around the table. "Very well!" The Colonel put his cue aside. "Let's get this matter over with."

≈ ≈ ≈ ≈ ≈

"You have been granted an audience, Mister Watkinson," the butler said. "If you will follow me?"

"Certainly, Mister er…?"

"Smithers, Sir. Just Smithers."

"Thank you, Smithers." Rodney stepped over the threshold, subconsciously straightening his tie and giving his jacket a smart tug at the hem. He followed Smithers to the drawing room, too busy with his thoughts to pay any attention to the interior décor of the Manor House.

"Madam?" Smithers found himself interrupting one of those interminable disputes he had been witness to the weary day long. "Sir?" The attention of his employers gained, he introduced the visitor. "Mister Watkinson."

"This had better be good, young man," the Colonel blustered as he bore down on him. "What is it? Vacuum cleaners? You look the salesman type." He looked him up and down as if he were something the dog had left underfoot.

Our hero set his jaw, he did not have to put up with this. The lady of the house stepped between the two as they came together; the older man red in the face, the younger pale and determined.

"Pleased to meet you, Mister Watkinson," Her Ladyship said, offering her hand. "Can we offer you something? Coffee perhaps?" The Colonel turned and stood a few steps away.

Rodney took a deep breath. "Coffee would be just the thing," he replied. He took another calming breath, shook Her Ladyship's hand. "Thank you, Mrs…. er… Your…?"

"Lady Brereton."

"Lady Brereton. Thank you. I came in connection with your daughter, Sir," Rodney said, turning, once more, to face the Colonel.

"So I understand. You'll excuse me if I don't shake your hand, Sir. It has been a very tiring day." He relented slightly. "It's been a very tiring day. Not usually so abrupt, what? Come in! Say your piece and be gone."

Her Ladyship led the way over to the armchairs set in the corner of the room, Smithers having already gone to fetch the coffee.

"You are at the bank I understand, Mister Watkinson?" she said, once the three were seated.

"That's right. Assistant Manager actually, Lady Bret…"

"Ma'am will serve, young man."

"Cuthbert! Please!"

"Ma'am," Rodney amended.

"You have been seeing my daughter, have you not, Mister Watkinson?"

"That's right, ma'am, yes. That's why I came to see you…"

"Tommy rot!" the Colonel barked. "We know all about it. Dash it all, the whole town knows. Don't know why you came here at all. Damnable cheek, that's what it is. Damnable cheek!"

"If I may, Cuthbert?"

"Harumph!"

"Thank you!" Her Ladyship returned her attention to Rodney. "Mister Watkinson, we do, as my husband noted, know all about it. However, I heard the story from Gillian herself." She looked over to the glowering Colonel. "Unlike some I could mention, I do not take for gospel every bit of gossip I happen to hear. Now, am I to understand that you have sufficient interest in my daughter to brave being set upon by the dogs? And I don't mean Redfers and Blackie." She gave a sidelong glance in the direction of the Colonel. "I mean my husband's dogs. If so, you are obviously more than the charlatan you are made out to be."

"Your Ladyship, I came here because I love your daughter and would like to know where she is. Why did she leave so suddenly? I can't really believe she would play me for a fool. Is she really engaged to a toffee… er… a toff? If you'll pardon me for asking?"

"Coffee is served, Madam." Smithers wheeled in the beverage trolley and made to start serving.

"Thank you, Smithers, we'll help ourselves."

"As you wish, Madam." The butler withdrew to a point just beyond the doorway.

Meanwhile, the Colonel had been biting his tongue, but now, face red as a turkey cock, he gave in to the inevitable.

"My daughter certainly is engaged, you cur! To a suitable young gentleman and I'll stand by for no more of this nonsense." He pulled himself to his feet. "Smithers!" he bellowed.

"Sir?" The butler strode back into the room.

"'Mister' Watkinson is just leaving. Shove him out… The back way." He glared at Rodney, face like fire, pointed with arm outstretched to the door. "Out! Before I do set my dogs upon you!"

Our hero was already on his feet, fists balled and at his sides. Her Ladyship, also standing, powerless now against her husband's wrath, said quietly, "I think you had best leave, Mister Watkinson. Perhaps another time?"

Rodney mentally counted to ten; relaxed himself with an effort. "Perhaps another time, yes," he said. He thought that maybe he should overturn the untouched coffee urn on his way out but decided he wouldn't give the Colonel the pleasure.

"This way, Mister Watkinson," the butler said.

He led off, Rodney striding along in his wake.

The Colonel was still huffing and puffing long after the pair had left.

"Thank you, Mister Smithers," Rodney called over his shoulder.

"Just Smithers, Sir. Just Smithers," the butler muttered tiredly as he closed the heavy door.

But Rodney was no longer listening. He took the stone steps two at a time, the butler having shown him out the way he had come in, Colonel's orders or no, and stomped across the courtyard to his waiting car. How anyone could be so rude to a guest he did not know. He stood by the side of his car, glaring back at the Manor House.

"Best leave it alone, lad!"

"What?" Rodney looked around for the source of the voice.

A man in later middle-age, looking dapper in a chauffeur's uniform approached. "I was just saying, best leave it alone. The name's Frank, lad. I'm the chauffeur here."

"Rodney Watkinson. I'm…"

"Aye! I know who you are, lad." Frank Rutter reached into a pocket and pulled out a pipe. "You came to ask about Miss Gillian I heard." He held the pipe by the bowl, but made no attempt to light it.

"That's right. Came to the front door in a civilized fashion and got treated like a…"

"Yes, the Colonel can be like that sometimes."

"Don't know who he thinks he is anyway, treating me like that. Wanted me shoved out the back door and loose his dogs on me."

"That's as maybe, but you have to remember that Miss Gillian is his only daughter. His only child come to that. Then, there he is, all set up for the big wedding and she runs off." Frank paused, pointed the end of his pipe in Rodney's direction and added, "Amid scandal and gossip, I might add."

"Yes, well..." Rodney looked down at his shoes, face reddening. "I can see he has a right to get worked up a bit but still, Lady Brereton was decent with me."

"Aye, well, that's her way, lad." The chauffeur stuck the end of the pipe into his mouth and spoke around it. "Don't know what we'd do without her sometimes, nor what we'll do without Miss Gillian for that matter." He removed the pipe from his mouth and pointed it at Rodney again. "You've other worries though if you want to win your young lady back and be welcome here."

"Meaning?"

Frank wagged the pipe end over his shoulder, waving it towards the Manor House. "Meaning Himself in there, the Colonel. You standing here glowering and plotting to get back at him will do you no good, lad. No good at all. Best leave things be, like I was saying. Just go about your business at the bank... Oh, aye, lad, like I was saying, I know who you are... and don't go getting any worse of a name for yourself than you already have."

He alternated chewing on the end of his pipe with pointing it at Rodney.

"Miss Gillian will be back, you mark my words, she'll be back. And when she does return, don't you think it would help if you were not a sworn enemy of her father?"

He placed a comradely hand on the younger man's shoulder, at the same time returning the pipe to his pocket.

"He's concerned about her, lad. Probably thinks you're one of them fortune hunters he's always going on about. And who can blame him? A good looking girl like that and her being so well off? Nothing personal, lad, that's just the way it is. May as well go have a couple of pints, lad. You'll get nowhere here tonight."

"Mister Rutter?"

"Frank, lad, Frank."

"Frank. Do you know why Gillian left like that? We were getting on so well and then the next thing I know, she's in tears. I come back from a weekend down the Smoke, there's a runny-ink letter for me and she's gone."

Frank removed his hand from the young man's shoulder.

"There's none of us understands women, lad, least of all myself and there's an old saying, 'Can't live with 'em; Can't live without 'em.' As for me, I've never been married. Always managed to buggar things up before I got that far."

"I see?" Rodney said, doubtfully.

"No, why things were right as rain one minute and then she's in tears the next, I couldn't say. Probably something as you didn't do, as opposed to something you did do. That's the way they are see, lad?"

"But where did she go, Frank? Can you answer me that?"

"Switzerland'd be my guess…"

"Switzerland? Does she have someone there? Family?"

"A banker, lad. She has a banker there."

"But? I thought she got engaged to a toffee… a toff. What's all this about a banker? Do you mean I'm not the only one in her life?"

The chauffeur shook his head and sighed. "I meant as that is where her fortune is, lad. Her old Grandpa Brereton left it to her, in trust. In a Swiss account. And she did get engaged to a toffee-nosed-get, if that's what you were going to say. Cedric Ponsomby-Smythe can certainly play that part when he wants to. I wouldn't worry too much about him though. Why Miss Gillian got herself engaged to him so suddenly I couldn't say, but it wasn't to be wed."

"Not to be wed? Then what?"

"The ways of women, lad. The ways of women. If I was you, I'd go have them couple of pints we were talking about, give your head a rest. Things'll look better in the morning most likely. Happen as you might even hear from her as we are all missing? You never know."

"Maybe," Rodney muttered.

The chauffeur clapped him on the shoulder. "That's the way, lad. By the way, Miss Gillian did confide in me as how taken she was with you. That night I dropped her off at the wine bar. Well, don't lose hope. Cheerio!" With that, Frank Rutter turned and strolled off into the night.

Rodney got into his car. He had a lot to think about. Meanwhile, he would take the chauffeur's advice and go get himself a couple of pints down the pub. He had had a hard day.

The Heiress and the Banker
Chapter Twelve
A Quiet Night Out on the Town

Roxanne sat on the bottom step of the stairs to put on her red high-heeled shoes.

"Where're you off to all tarted up, ower Roxy?"

She stood up, looking every inch the... well, every inch the Roxanne Smith. Short black skirt, red silk blouse, black sheer stockings and the aforementioned red high-heeled shoes. Her black shoulder length hair was brushed out and tied back with a red ribbon. "Down Middlewich for a quiet drink," she said. "I've 'ad a rotten day if you must know, ower Andrea." She smoothed her skirt over her thighs.

"So I 'eard. I told you as that bank manager friend of yours was all of a do over Miss Rich Britches didn't I? Well, serve 'im right that she scarpered I say. You didn't go tellin' 'im what we saw on Satdee night did you, Roxanne? You've done yourself no favours if you 'ave. They used to shoot the bearers of bad news you know."

They were standing in the small space that served as an entrance hall.

"Well I did tell 'im and now I'm supposed to wear trouser suits at work. What do I want with a trouser suit? I'd 'ave been better off if 'e 'ad shot me."

"Oh, it's not that bad. We can go t' th' market if you like. I'll 'elp you look. Or would you rather borrow my Rupert trousers?"

"You mean those 'orrible things with all the different coloured squares? No thanks!"

"Well, it's only a suggestion, but I would advise you..."

"Piss off, Andrea. I don't need your advice after th' kind o' day as I've just 'ad. I'm off out." Roxanne stamped out and slammed the front door behind her. "Tarra!"

"Tarra!" Andrea said to the door. She pulled it open and stepped outside. "I would 'ave come with you, ower Roxy if you 'adn't been so rude," she shouted. "Tommy was askin' about you again today."

Roxanne turned around. "Piss off, Andrea!" she repeated, then was on her way.

"'old up, Roxanne." Andrea shoved her feet into her running shoes and set off in pursuit of her little sister. "I'll come with you." She was dressed in jeans and a halter top. Good enough for a quiet drink down Middlewich. "Wait up!" she called out then, under her breath, "Why you won't give Tommy a chance, I don't know. Plenty o' girls'd give their best high-heels to go out with 'im."

"What's up, Andrea?" Roxanne said when her sister had caught up. "Frightened you might miss summat?"

"Don't be like that, our Roxy. We'll eye up some proper talent. Never mind that Cockney."

"Yeah, you're right," Roxanne said. "There's plenty more fish in th' sea."

"Bigger ones than that'n as well, I dare say."

The sun finally broke out from behind a stray cloud, its golden rays filling the girls with all the joys of Spring. They were both giggling as they rounded the bottom of the avenues. "Tommy was askin' again did you say?"

≈ ≈ ≈ ≈ ≈

The Austin's front tyres scrabbled to get a purchase on the loose stones of the Manor Drive as Rodney, with heavy foot, pulled away. He headed straight for Middlewich and the 'White Boar', the lights at the aqueduct, as always, against him.

Once at the pub, he parked in his usual spot and went around to the front door. Although he had often thought about it, our hero had never yet been inside this particular establishment. One of the few remaining black and white timbered buildings in the town, it had often caught his eye. A few of the local men were propping up the bar when he entered.

"What'll it be, young fella?" the landlord asked jovially.

"Oh… er…?" Rodney scanned the generous array of pumps at the bar. Several brew makers names were displayed on the pump handles, however, his eyes were drawn to one particular pump, for no particular reason.

"A pint of your Potters' Best, please, landlord."

A sharp intake of breath from those assembled.

"You know your ale you do, lad," the landlord said. "Nice suit by the way."

"Thanks!" Rodney discreetly pulled down at the front of his trousers. Despite Rowena's careful measuring, they were a little tight around where it mattered most and, the pressure of the visit to the Manor House subsiding a little, he was now feeling the pinch.

"I was told earlier on that I looked like a vacuum cleaner salesman."

"Had a go at that once myself," one of the locals said.

"Aye! And I bought on of the buggers off you an' all, Harry. Bloody thing never was any good. My Missus harped on about it for ages."

The landlord planted a frothing pint pot of ale on the bar.

"There y'are, me old son. Get that down you."

Rodney reached for the pint pot.

"That'll be thirty pence, lad."

Another sharp intake of breath, this time from Rodney. However, he wasn't here to argue the toss. He pulled out a twenty pound note from his wallet.

"Inflammatory times, lad," the landlord said. "And that's a special brew. Ever tried it before?"

"Obviously not," Harry muttered.

"Not 'til now," Rodney said. "Cheers!" He had a thirst to quench and he meant to quench it.

"Cheers!" The rest of the company took a swallow with our hero.

"We've a pottery works the other side o' town," the landlord continued. "Hard drinking lads they are. That brew's named for them."

"I see!" Rodney took another good pull from his pint.

"Local brew it is."

"Aye! Made in Bill's bloody cellar, lad."

"The name's Bill, by the way," The Landlord said, ignoring Harry's remark. He handed Rodney his change. "And go easy with that stuff, me old son. It's bloody potent it is."

"Does have a bit of a kick to it," Rodney said then, after another swallow of ale, "Don't hear that one often 'Me old son'. Not up here anyway. More like down the Smoke that."

"Aye, well, I was down there just after the war… mind how you sup that, young fella, it's bloody potent it is… that's where I met the Missus."

Harry and his mate wandered over to a table; they'd heard Bill's 'Just after the war' tales and thought he was about to wax lyrical on the subject. They were wrong though; it was Rodney who had a story to tell on this night.

"Oh, yes?" Our hero took another pull from his pint. He'd set the change from the twenty on the bar top and had no intentions of pocketing it.

"Yes, met the Missus there… and there's many a time as I've wished I'd o' never seen the place."

"You didn't like London then?"

"Been stood up?" The Landlord said, suddenly changing the subject.

"What?"

"It's none o' my business like, but you look like you got all done up and she didn't show. I know I'm a nosey bugger, but I'm right aren't I lad, I'm right?"

"Put another pint in there," our hero said, placing his empty pot firmly on the bar counter's polished top, "and I might tell you."

"Right you are, lad!" The landlord swept the ale pot up, refilled it and set it back down in place. All in one swift movement.

"That'll be thirty pence."

Rodney indicated for him to help himself to the correct amount from the money on the bar top. "One for yourself?"

"Don't mind if I have half, lad. And take it a bit easier with this one, lad. Potter's Best is bloody potent it bloody well is."

By the time that Rodney was halfway down his third pint (and Bill was on his second half) the story was beginning to make sense.

"So you're that bloke?" the landlord said.

"That's shright!" Rodney replied, by now three sheets to the wind. "That bloche! And zshat twenchy I gave ya? Thash wiz zshat twenchy!" He downed the remainder of the ale and slammed the empty pot on the bar. "Landslorch! Anusher pyant… poleze!"

The landlord pulled another pint, the Londoner was certainly livening up a normally quiet night. Meanwhile, Harry and his mate sat ears cocked at the dominoes table.

"There y'are, young fella!" The landlord thought that maybe he should have persuaded him to stop at three. "And take it easy with this one, lad." He placed a fresh frothing pint at Rodney's elbow.

"That bloody stuff's bloody well potent it bloody well is. Stronger than that Pie-Eyed Parson as they sell at the 'Newtown

Brewery' it is. Although I dare say as old Albert'd argue the toss on that one."

Rodney took a pull from the refilled pot. "Albish?" he said, spilling some of his Potter's Best as he set the ale pot down.

"Albert, lad. The landlord at the 'Newtown Brewery'. You were saying, lad?"

"Wash I?"

"Young Miss Gillian… and that…"

"Oh, yesh, well… She tooksh me inshto the woodsh…"

≈ ≈ ≈ ≈ ≈

Roxanne and her sister had had a couple of drinks in the 'Vaulters' Arms' but had now grown tired of the place. It being, like most places of entertainment in Middlewich on a Monday night, almost empty.

"Come on, ower kid! Sup up, we'll go to th' 'White Boar' for a change. Who knows, maybe Tommy'll show up?"

"Andrea, 'ave you set me up? Because if you 'ave…!"

"Ah, ah!" Andrea sprang to her feet. "No you don't." She tipped the bottoms of her drink down her throat, dumped the glass onto the table and headed for the door. Her sister was in hot pursuit.

They ran out onto the street just as the church clock started to chime the hour of ten o' clock.

"Come on, our Roxy! I'll race ya."

"What? And me in me 'igh 'eels?"

≈ ≈ ≈ ≈ ≈

"Gushnight, mein hosht… I shall reshurn!" Our hero started to weave his way out of the pub. "I shall shry… try… shum ofs shat Pissed-Up-Parson…?"

"Pie-Eyed-Parson," Bill corrected.

"Pied-Parshon you menshunshed. 'Newt and Brewery' dish you shay?"

"'Newtown Brewery', me old son… and mind how you go. It's down Pepper Lane."

The landlord of the 'White Boar' shook his head in dismay. He doubted that young Rodney would make it down the front steps in one piece, never mind to the other end of Pepper Lane. Well, he would have to manage. Bill himself had had to often enough in the past and at least he had been able to persuade Rodney to hand his car keys over. If he did make it to the 'Newtown Brewery' and back, Bill had decided to give him a room for the night. He didn't do much business that way and it would cost him nothing; and there was no way he was going to give him his car keys back. Not while he was in that state. Still, the young fellow deserved a good night out after what he'd been through, but let him stagger about on foot… or all fours.

Bill shook his head and tut-tutted. 'Pie-Eyed Parson' on top of 'Potter's Best'? "Mind that step now, lad!"

Our hero gave a lop-sided grin before teetering down the steps… right into the arms of Roxanne Smith.

"Mith Thmith?" he said, trying to maintain his balance. "Wash a shurprize!" He untangled himself from her arms and tottered about foolishly.

"Oh? Mister Watkinson? Are you all right?"

"e's drunk," Andrea said. "Just look at 'im. Done up like a vacuum cleaner salesman and pissed as a fart. Pitiful."

"And you, Masham," Rodney began, addressing his remarks to Roxanne, "are a delectashable… deshetalable… tasty tart busht, in the morninsh, I shall shtill be drrruunk! An' you shall shtill be a tarsht!"

"Come on, ower Roxy!" Andrea said. "Forget 'im." She started up the steps to the pub. "It's your round an' all."

"Jusht a minish, Roxshanne…" Rodney barred her way. "Wash culid undies are ya wearinsh tonishe, you lishle teasher?"

"There not any colour, Mister Watkinson," she said, forgetting they were no longer at the bank. "Not any colour at all."

"Nosh wearinsh any?" Our hero (though I'm not sure we should still be referring to him thus) threw one arm around Roxanne's shoulders while the other shot under her skirt.

Roxanne was flabbergasted. First a drunken speech, now this? She galvanized herself into action, bringing her arms down scissor fashion to trap Rodney's forearm.

As far as she knew, she had never even got a rise out of her boss before. Now, here he was, in the middle of the street, going for first prize.

Rodney staggered back in confusion; Roxanne's handbag strap slid from her shoulder down to her wrist.

"Roxshanne? I jusht washed to sheck out your undiesh…!"

Andrea came back down the steps in two strides. "You leave my sister alone, you oaf!" She prepared her own handbag for a pre-emptive strike, but no need… Roxanne's was there first. When her bag had arrived at her wrist, she took the strap in a firm grasp and swung it at her molester's head.

"Wosh the blooshy 'ell?" Rodney started to keel over, one hand to the side of his head.

Not to be outdone, Andrea lumped him another good one while he was on his way down. Job done, she and her sister stomped up the steps and into the pub. Our fallen hero was thus left to his own devices.

"Blushy wimin!" he muttered as he got clumsily to his feet. "Cansh live wiv 'em… Peppup Lane is it? Pished up Parshon. Shee wot Albish has to shay."

And so, Rodney Watkinson, on his second week in Middlewich and the boring north, weaved his drunken way around the

'Vaulters' Arms' towards the four lanes of the expressway. Pepper Lane was on the opposite side of the road.

Evenin', girls! What'll it be tonight?"

"Two 'alfs of lager please, Bill."

Harry and his mate pushed the dominoes aside and came over to lean on the bar.

"Me and my mate'll try a pint each of your 'Potter's Best', when you're ready, Bill."

"All in good time, Harry." The landlord took two half-pots from the clean tray and filled them from the lager pump. "What does the other girl look like?" he asked, placing the filled glasses on the bar.

"What girl?"

"You look like you've been in a tussle, young Roxanne. I was just saying, what does the other girl look like?"

"You're just a nosey bugger, Bill." Andrea pushed herself in front of her younger sister and handed him a fifty pence piece from her purse. "And we're not telling. What's all this?"

"All what?"

"All this money lyin' about 'ere." She picked up several soggy banknotes and some loose change off a beer mat.

"Well I'll be buggered… That young fella forgot to pick it up. He'll be back, happen. You must know him, Roxanne. Works at the bank."

"Thar know's as she knows 'im, Bill," Harry said, a twinkle in his eye.

"Yes, I know 'im," Roxanne said glumly. She turned to her sister. "I 'ave to go to 'im, ower Andrea. I can't just leave 'im lyin' there like that."

"Don't be daft, ower Roxy…"

But Roxanne had already run headlong out the door. Her feet touched pavement on Wheelock Street at exactly the right moment for her to hear the screeching of tyres from the direction of the expressway. Rodney was nowhere to be seen.

Something heavy slammed to a halt with a sickening thump.

"Rodney? Nooooooo!" She kicked off her high-heeled shoes and ran down the street. Headlong she ran, around the 'Vaulters Arms', to be greeted by the sight she had been dreading.

A double-decker bus, nose in to the concrete keep left bollard, standing at a crazy angle; traffic at a standstill on both sides of the expressway… and a body lying inert on the central reservation.

"Rodney! Noooooo!" she screamed anew. She ran over to him. "Oh, no! No! Noo!"

Someone else was already on the scene.

"Roxanne?"

It was all too much. She collapsed in tears; Tommy Boyle caught her before she could hit the ground.

The Heiress and the Banker
Chapter Thirteen
The Grand Finale

Gillian was in trouble. Real trouble! It was not so much the fact that for the past three months she had been getting steadily bigger around the waist. She had come to terms with that long since. Our heroine was in fact quite looking forward to becoming a mother with a daughter of her own to look after. And Gillian was certain that the child she carried would be a girl. Just as certain as she was that the child was Rodney's. Her intuition told her. That and the fact that Cedric had had the foresight to wear a protective all those months ago; and Rodney Blue Eyes had not.

As for Peter Smith well, by that time she had already been well and truly pregnant. She had had to get back to England and she had only two assets left. Even the ring that Cedric had presented her with had had to go. And then Peter Smith had come along; he'd been so sweet, and lots of girls did it just for fun. Gillian had needed money and there was no way she would ever sell TRemor.

That little episode was behind her now, she was back in the land of her birth. No more gambling; no more silliness… and no more the heiress. She was flat broke; pregnant and determined to be an ordinary young woman. She would get a job; she would find a way to bring up her baby. When she was ready, she would return to her parents' home… but she wanted to overcome her troubles first.

Then there was the matter of Rodney; she still loved him. But she would decide what to do about him later. Meanwhile, she had a purpose in life; she would get a job and be useful to society.

Useful out of necessity yes but, ironically, it was what she had wanted. Besides, most ordinary young women got a job and became useful to society out of necessity. So, in a fashion, she had attained her dearest wish; to become ordinary.

Problems like Gillian's, pregnant and a blown inheritance, out of touch with her loved ones, she still thought she could handle… in time and with a bit of luck. Our heroine's immediate problem, however, was just that, immediate!

"Come on, old girl! Don't give up on me now. We've come this far, it's just a little further. Just a little further."

The TR5, Gillian's beloved roadster, was not running well at all. The car had had a job to climb that last hill… and each successive hill that she encountered hereabouts seemed to be steeper than the one before. She gripped the wheel tightly and peered out at the rain-shrouded hills. Low hills, but imposing in their bleakness, they seemed to crowd in from either side.

"Just a little further!" she repeated, mantra fashion. "Just a little further."

Gillian knew that if she did not get to somewhere soon, she would be stranded. Our heroine knew what the problem was or, more properly, the symptoms. Mis-firing! She had been listening to it steadily worsen since she had left the M62. At that time, within easy reach of help, Gillian had denied the existence of the problem. Now it was undeniable. It had got so bad that her hands were going numb from hanging on to the vibrating steering wheel. Then there was the temperature gauge; Gillian had never seen it climb so high.

A winding road; another hill. Our heroine slammed her foot down on the throttle pedal hoping, perhaps, to gain momentum. The straight six coughed, backfired… and stalled. Gillian steered the car back down the hill and onto the grass verge. She cranked the engine over, but there was no way that it would restart.

Gillian slumped back in her seat. Rain lashed the windows of the car; the wind whistled around the seals of the fabric top. She was stranded. Not only that, she was lost. Lost, but not beaten. Our heroine had been through too much of late to allow herself to be beaten now.

"Just have to walk!" she decided resolutely. "If only I had a map."

Our heroine did in fact have a map; a Michelin Route Map… of France.

She had tried to consult it earlier when she first realized that she was lost (the narrow winding roads of Yorkshire were not like the Motorway) and had tossed it behind the seats in disgust. She slapped the steering wheel and uttered an oath… she felt like crying, but she would not. She would walk, to somewhere, and that was that.

≈ ≈ ≈ ≈ ≈

Rodney settled back into the overstuffed armchair, placed his cup of tea on the side table and rested his feet up against the hearth. He was away for the weekend (and obviously not dead) at Mrs. Bayley's B&B.

"You get yourself comfortable, Mister Watkinson…"

"Rodney, please."

"Aye well, Rodney then. I was just sayin', it's a bad night out there. Wouldn't want to be at large in this I wouldn't. It's a good… I say, it's a good thing as you put your motorbike in the shed isn't it?"

"You're right there, Mrs. Bayley." Rodney had brought his bike up from London once he had got properly settled in Middlewich.

"Very snug you'll find this room, Mister Watkinson," Mrs. Bayley went on, pulling the parlour room drapes tightly across the window. "Very snug! Walls a foot thick this 'ouse 'as got. Good Yorkshire stone as well. They don't build 'em like this anymore they don't."

"Yes, it does seem a stout place, Mrs. Bayley," Rodney replied. Not for the first time, he looked around the room. "You've a nice bit of brass as well. Must take some polishing?"

"Ohhh, yes!" his hostess replied, bustling over to the fireplace. "Wednesday's me brass polishin' day… Ease your feet up, love…. Keeps me out o' trouble it does."

Rodney pulled his feet back from the brass rail and watched as the elderly Mrs. Bayley stoked up the fire. He would have offered to help, but had tried that earlier; his hostess had steadfastly refused. He was a paying guest; she was the hotelier.

"Eeh! I'll be gettin' old yet!" Mrs. Bayley exclaimed, straightening up from her duties. She held a hand to the small of her back. "It's all this damp weather we've been 'avin'. Does me back no good at all and then tomorrow's me market day and just listen to it outside." She supported herself with one hand on the mantelpiece.

Rodney got to his feet. "Please! Mrs. Bayley… Sit down and I'll pour you a nice cup of tea. You'll allow me that small pleasure, surely?"

Mrs. Bayley eased herself down into the armchair opposite to the fire from Rodney's while he poured the tea. "You're a thoughtful young chap, Mister Watkinson… Rodney," she said, taking the cup from his hand. "Very thoughtful… Eeh, me back… It's a wonder that you 'aven't been snapped up long since by some lass. I dare say, 'owever, as you've a string of 'em somewhere."

Rodney settled himself into the armchair once more. "I dare say as I've had my moments," he replied. He took a sip of his tea and stared into the flickering flames beyond the hearth rail.

Mrs. Bayley waited. It was a perfect night for a story of romance and intrigue. "Do you still love 'er, Rodney?" she prompted.

Our heroine climbed out of her roadster, not so nimbly as she had been used to in the past but still, she was not all that big yet. She hurriedly got into her flapping raincoat, her hair already plastered against her head. The car was up against a dry-stone wall, park brake firmly applied and second gear engaged. She locked the doors and the boot, not that there was much in the latter, and set off.

Raincoat pulled tightly around her, head bent to the wind, Gillian trudged up the road. Apart from herself, there was not a soul about. It was more like the back end of winter than a late July evening.

"Brrr!" Gillian shivered and clutched the raincoat more tightly about herself. "How far to 'Brigadoon'?" she muttered.

Despite her encouraging words to TRemor, our heroine really did not know how far she was from civilization. All she knew was that she was somewhere on the high moorlands of Yorkshire, alone!

Our heroine, Miss Gillian Brereton-Holbeck had been through a lot of living since her presence had last graced the shores of the British Isles. Firstly, there had been Switzerland with its magnificent views, yodeling ski-instructors… and Schnapps.

Gillian had had to go to that picturesque little country anyway; the numbered account and, with it, her maternal grandfather's bequest were both in Switzerland. So, why not stay for a while and enjoy the sights?

It was in Switzerland that she had first realized that she was with child. Skiing was much too strenuous of an activity for a girl in her condition so she had moved on to Monte Carlo, her original destination. She would enjoy the sun, the beaches and fashion. She would straighten her feelings out; get her emotions in order, then return to the land of her birth. Once there, she would use her inheritance to buy a cosey cottage for herself and her baby, invite her parents round and put things right. Prodigals were supposed to get forgiven, weren't they? Then there was Rodney of the Blue Eyes. How to handle him? She still loved him. Would he now love her for the baby's sake? Had he loved her in the first place for the money? She couldn't answer every question at once; first she had to find herself.

Yes, it had been a fine plan… but, there was that little word 'If'.

If the casinos had not been so inviting; if her new 'friends' had not been so encouraging; Gillian might still have her inheritance.

Well, if and but not withstanding, all her money had run out. She had been stranded in the South of France, without money or friends. Her new 'friends' had disappeared as quickly as that which had attracted them in the first place. Our heroine would not appeal to her parents, she was too proud for that. That was when Peter Smith had come along.

Peter Smith; rugged, weather-beaten, somewhat older and oddly sweet in his concern. A night of mutual comfort and warmth; a coffee and croissant the following morning; a gift… and it had all been over. Our heroine had accepted the gift without objection, she understood the implications, but did not dwell on the matter.

She had been in need of money… it had been a gift. She was solvent again. Solvent enough to get back to Blighty at least and, at the time, that was all that mattered.

Back to Blighty, but not the environs of Occles-Leigh or Middlewich. She had given those places a wide berth. She was not ready to face her parents yet. She would see them again, yes… but not with cap in hand. The same went for Rodney. Rodney of the Blue Eyes; she still loved him. Could he ever forgive her? Rodney! Were he and that Jezebel an item now?

"'Jezebel'?" Gillian muttered. "If anyone's a Jezebel it's me." She paced on. "I… am… what… I… am!" she said aloud, marking time as she sloshed along. "I… am… what… I… am."

Rodney finished his story and stared bleakly at the glowing coals. Mrs. Bayley was a kind old soul, she reminded him of his mum, and Rodney had wanted to talk of Gillian. Something he hadn't done in a long while.

"And you've never 'eard of 'er since?"

Rodney shook himself out of his reverie and turned to face his hostess. "Oh, it's nothing, Mrs. Bayley," he lied. He picked up his tea cup and took a sip. The tea had long since gone cold. "I'm sorry I bothered you with it."

He got to his feet and placed his cup and saucer on the tray with the other tea things. "I did hear that the other chap, the one she was engaged to, got hooked up with someone else. And word did go around that Gillian had gone to Switzerland."

"She's been in touch with somebody then?"

"Not that I know of. There was something about her parents being told she had taken her inheritance from a bank there. Cleared out the account."

"A young woman abroad with a fortune burnin' 'oles in 'er 'andbag?" Mrs. Bayley furrowed her brow. "Well, the path of true love never did run smooth, young Rodney." One hand pressed against the arm of the chair, the other at the small of her back, she eased herself to her feet. "If you don't mind me sayin' so," she puffed, "it's obvious you're still in love with 'er." She peered at the mantel clock. "Eeh 'eck! Just look at th' time. 'ow it flies." She placed a gentle hand on Rodney's forearm. "You'll see 'er again, never fear. I feel it in me bones, I do. Well, I'll clean up 'ere, Mister Watkinson," she said, suddenly all business. "If there's owt else you want, just 'elp yourself. You know where the kitchen is. Watch th' telly if you like, but there's blessed little on these days. I'm off to bed meself."

Rodney stepped out of the way. "Goodnight, Mrs. Bayley. I'll probably turn in myself soon. An early night wouldn't hurt."

"Goodnight then. Bank th' fire up before you go up will you? It doesn't do to leave it flarin'."

"I will, Mrs. Bayley, don't you worry about that."

Mrs. Bayley paused in the process of leaving the parlour. She looked at him, tray in her hands. "Don't worry about your Gillian, Rodney. I'm sure she loves you. She'll come back, you mark an old woman's words."

Rodney did not answer, he merely turned away.

"I'll put an 'ot water bottle in for you," Mrs. Bayley said. She then turned away and left her guest to his own affairs.

≈ ≈ ≈ ≈ ≈

It seemed to Gillian that she was forever struggling up hill and the wind, the wind was forever in her face no matter which way the road turned. She had no idea how far the nearest town or village was and she was already soaked to the skin. She had given up trying to hold her raincoat down against the blow of the gale long since, that had only proven to be an exercise in frustration. She felt miserable, dejected, cold and hungry. Gillian had not been prepared for anything like this, she was still dressed for the South of France. Her raincoat, however fashionable, was never meant to actually keep the rain out. Her lightweight sweater was wet and worse than useless. It only served to hold water and chill her even more. Then there were her feet. Her feet squelched with every step. However, Gillian would not be beaten now. She would not give up.

Rodney could find nothing of interest on the television and he did not feel like venturing out to the local pub. Not with a storm raging like the one tonight. He'd had enough of the elements for one day riding up to Yorkshire on his trusty old Thunderbird and so decided to take his own advice. He climbed the stairs. Up to bed for an early night.

"Bah!" he muttered. He had planned on sleeping with something a bit more lively than a hot water bottle. Rodney, in love with Gillian though he was, had planned on sleeping with that little sex siren at the bank.

He had planned on sleeping with the girl that had put the tease back into tease. Rodney had planned on sleeping with our very own Roxanne Smith.

Our hero went about his nightly ablutions, climbed into bed, got comfortable between the sheets and closed his eyes. Yes, he loved Gillian with all his heart and soul, but he was not a monk.

And so, he had planned on a dirty weekend with Roxanne. The two of them had developed an understanding; they were now firm friends. Rodney had been surprised, not to mention disappointed, at her refusal.

≈ ≈ ≈ ≈ ≈

Rodney's one true love felt like she had been walking forever when, drenched, footsore and weary, she came at last to a village.

"'Stow-on-the-Moors'," she read aloud. Gillian rested thankfully against the village sign.

"At last!" she sighed. "At long last." She started to doze in the persistent heavy rain until… the local church clock began to chime the hour.

"One… Two… Three?" Gillian repeated aloud. "It can't be!" She pulled back her sodden sleeve and peered at her watch. It was useless, the face was so steamed up that she couldn't make out the hands. "I could have at least hung on to my Rolex," she thought miserably, shoving her sleeve back into place.

Apart from the few street lamps, all in the village was in darkness. Our heroine pushed herself away from the sign and pressed on.

"Everyone must be tucked up in bed," she thought, shivering. "All tucked up and warm in bed."

And that, tucked up and warm in bed, was precisely where Gillian wanted to be. Tucked up and warm in bed. She splashed on, almost in tears.

≈ ≈ ≈ ≈ ≈

Our hero, of course, was tucked up and warm in bed. He had been for several hours. However, tucked up and warm in bed though he was, he was not asleep. Rodney was wide awake. He could not get his mind off Roxanne Smith. His thoughts were making him uncomfortable. Several times, in his frustration, he had bashed his pillow. Still, he was unable to get to sleep.

He turned his mind to the events of three months earlier, the time he had almost lost his life under that double-decker bus. He could remember his visit to the Manor House, and he could remember going into the 'White Boar' shortly afterwards. He could even remember, vaguely, attempting to fondle Miss Smith outside that establishment. But he'd be damned if he could remember anything of that night after that. He'd been told, several times, that a local character by the name of Tommy Boyle had saved his life.

Tommy, it seems, had been coming out from the 'Crown and Anchor' by the church when he had seen a drunk attempting to cross the expressway. The drunk had made it across the first two lanes but there was a bus hammering down the road from the direction of North Wilderspool. Now Tommy knew a bit about drunks, from first hand experience, and he could see that this one would never make it across the road. He had not hesitated. A quick look for traffic and he had sprinted across the road, shoulder charging the said drunk and knocking him flat on the central reservation; thus saving Rodney's life. The bus, luckily, had not been carrying any passengers as it was out of service and returning to the depot. The driver had been shook up but not hurt.

Tommy had earned Rodney's eternal thanks that day and, apparently, had become Roxanne's hero.

After that, Rodney had managed to pull himself together. He'd been given a week off work; stress leave and, during this time, had got busy putting his affairs in order. He had found a nice place to live and was now the lodger of Mrs. McKenzie, a resident of Pepper Lane. He'd also found time to visit London and his mum, this time going by train. After that short visit, he had returned riding his old Thunderbird.

He had then bought an how to book for his Austin 1100 and done some tinkering. Then, and perhaps most importantly, he had thrown himself at his work. As a result of this, he had made the right kind of impression in the right place. Upon Mister Snoddlegrass's retirement (the old banker had reportedly moved to Spain with Brunhilde) Rodney had become the new manager of Avonlea's Bank, Middlewich.

His thoughts then drifted to how he had planned his weekend away. A weekend of biking, hiking on the moors… and that. He had scoured a B&B brochure and decided on this village; tucked away at the back of beyond. He had phoned Mrs. Bayley in advance. In advance, but only after Miss Smith had refused his offer.

The new assistant manager was one Melvin Ashwood, lately of the Birmingham branch. Rodney remembered putting his head around the door of his own former office.

"When our Miss Smith returns from lunch, Mister Ashwood, could you ask her to step into my office, please?"

"Certainly, Mister Watkinson," the harried looking Mister Ashwood had replied. (Roxanne had not had to suffer the indignity of going to work in a trouser suit. Mister Snoddlegrass had overruled that decision saying that it would be cruel and unusual punishment. Mrs. Davies had raised her eyebrows, but Mister Snoddlegrass had been the boss. Rodney had since learned to live with the decision.) "She does have an appointment with me shortly after lunch, but certainly I will send her your way first." (Mister Ashwood, however, was new to the territory.)

Rodney had returned to his own office. Mrs. McKenzie supplied him with a packed lunch so, these days, he ate at his desk. He had been finishing off his cuppa when there was a tap at the door. Miss Smith, as punctual as ever.

Mister Watkinson leaned back in his chair and got comfortable, the chair opposite the desk having already been moved back a little. Miss Smith still liked him to have a good view. "Entrée!" he called out exuberantly.

The door swung open and Roxanne Smith entered with a flourish. She stood, door closed, right hand on the knob, sideways on to Rodney. She placed her left hand on her hip, adopted a wide-legged stance and smiled sweetly in her Manager's direction. That day, she had been wearing an ankle length black cotton skirt, the split (in the side facing Rodney) ran from the hem to just above her stocking tops.

Miss Smith lifted the sunglasses from in front of her eyes, placed them on the top of her head and winked mischievously.

"You wanted to see me, Mister Watkinson?" she purred, making her way to the well placed office chair.

"Yes, I did, Miss Smith. It's a personal matter."

"Oh, yes?" Roxanne breathed. She sat down, one leg crossed over the other. She pulled the flowing skirt from around her knees.

"Yes, Miss Smith." Rodney loosened his tie. Roxanne never failed to raise his blood pressure and this visit had been no exception. She sat, legs crossed and skirt fallen open. Black stilettos, sheer stockings over shapely legs, red frilly garter belt with underwear to match. All were in full view.

"Ahh! Roxanne, you're a tease. Promise me you'll never change."

"There's no chance of that, Rodney," Miss Smith replied. "No chance of me changing, that is." She ran her tongue around her lips and repositioned her legs. Her left ankle was now resting on her right knee.

"What did you want to see me about, sweetheart?" Roxanne asked, undoing a blouse button. Her bra, low cut and, like her underwear and garter belt, red, did not disappoint.

"Well, Roxanne." Rodney paused to take a gulp from his water glass (he always kept one on hand when Miss Smith was visiting these days). "How would you like to come away for the weekend? With me? We'll go biking and hiking… and that… on the moors. Stay at a B&B. All respectable, of course."

"Well, of course it would be respectable, Mister Watkinson." Roxanne got to her feet and buttoned up her blouse. Rodney had had his treat and she had an appointment to keep with the new assistant manager. "But I'm sorry, love. I have to say no. If you'd have asked me a few weeks ago, I might have said yes, but not now."

Rodney had not been expecting this. He got to his feet. "Is it something I've said, Roxanne?"

Miss Smith looked him in the eye. "Rodney, you've always been a gentleman with me… apart from that one time… and I dare say as I've tempted you a time or two. No, it's not something you've said, or done for that matter. But we have to consider our professional relationship."

"Professional relationship?" Rodney gasped.

"Yes and besides, I'm going steady."

"Well, I'm very happy for you," Rodney mumbled.

"Come off it, Rodney. You still love Miss Rich Britches, we both know that. A dirty weekend with you would have been nice, even a respectable one. But you would have regretted it. Besides, I'm not that kind of a girl."

"Not that kind of a girl?" Rodney spluttered.

"Of course not!" Roxanne said. "I'm like you said, a tease. The man that beds me must wed me first. It drives Tommy crazy, but that's how it is."

Rodney had taken another gulp of water. Surprising news indeed. "Roxanne, I... I don't know what to say. I wish you and Tommy all the best."

Roxanne took one of his hands in hers and tickled his palm. "Thank you!" She let go of Rodney's hand. "I'd better get next door now. Mister Ashwood is expecting me."

"Yes, quite."

Roxanne placed her hands on her hips and tossed her hair. "I think it is the dress code, Mister Watkinson."

Rodney put one foot on his chair and, with elbow on knee and chin in hand, looked thoughtful. "I did hear there have been some changes, Miss Smith."

"I know," Roxanne purred.

He looked at her quizzically. "Length of skirt?" he queried.

"Knee length or longer," Miss Smith replied.

"Colour of clothing, etc.?"

"Sober, good quality... as before."

"Mmm! I see..." He stood more upright, now with hand on knee, as he asked, "And scarlet red underwear, Miss Smith?"

Roxanne had not even hesitated. "None of your business, Mister Watkinson. A gentleman would avert his gaze."

"Very good, Roxanne, very good." He had then changed his stance in order to lean over the desk, weight resting on his hands.

"And the split up the side of your skirt, Miss Smith?" he demanded.

Roxanne had tossed her hair again and laughed. "Not mentioned in the dress code at all, Mister Watkinson. Not mentioned at all."

"Excellent!" Rodney said. "Excellent!" He had then walked around the desk to escort Miss Smith out of his office. He opened the door with a flourish and gestured for the young trainee to exit.

"Why, thank you, kind sir!" Roxanne chirruped. She curtsied. "Thank you very much." With that, she put her new sunglasses back into place and swished out of the room.

"Oh, Miss Smith!"

"Yes?" Roxanne had paused to look around.

"Go easy on the lad won't you?"

Roxanne had raised her sunglasses, winked and replied in her best sultry tone, "You know me, Mister Watkinson. I always go easy."

So, as far as Rodney was concerned, that was that. His one true love had left him; he'd missed the boat with the entrancing Miss Smith. Now, here he lay, alternately bashing his pillow and trying to sleep.

Into the night he whispered, "Roxanne is right. I do love you, Gillian... and by all that I hold sacred, I always will."

The village clock started to chime the hour. The third and last stroke was still reverberating as our hero fell into a deep and dreamless sleep.

Our heroine trudged through Stow-on-the-Moors, seeking refuge from the night. There! A dim light in a porch. Gillian did not think twice. She was up the path, front gate still swinging on its hinges, and slapping desperately on the front door knocker. She was on the point of collapse when the door opened.

"Eeeh, 'eck, love!"

Gillian felt a motherly arm around her; she was inside. The door closed; she heard the bolt go across. Our heroine was safe.

≈ ≈ ≈ ≈ ≈

Sunlight streaming through a window; a snug feeling of well-being. Gillian's eyes opened and she looked around, trying to put a name to her surroundings.

Memory flooded back. Her drive up from Dover the day before; the wind and the rain; TRemor breaking down. Her long and weary walk over the moors in the pouring rain. Then the village and the old lady's cottage.

A knock on the door. "Are you awake, love?"

"Yes, come in." Gillian kicked the eiderdown back and sat up on the couch.

The old lady entered the parlour carrying a cup of tea. "I 'ope you like it sweet, love. It'll do you no 'arm after what you must 'ave gone through, turning up on me doorstep like a 'alf drowned rat an' all. Larks a mercy, it's a wonder you 'aven't caught yourself pneumonia on top of everything else. Well, it's to be 'oped you're feelin' a bit better this mornin', it is."

Gillian looked down at herself. She was wearing a pair of baggy flannel pyjamas; presumably a pair of the old lady's. She took hold of the cup.

"This is very kind of you, Mrs.…?"

"Well, 'ere's me prattlin' on and we haven't even been introduced. All I could think of last night was to get you in and dry. It's Mrs. Bayley, love. Used to guests I am. I'll not be chargin' you a penny though, not a girl in your straits I won't."

"I'm not in any position to argue with that, Mrs. Bayley. My name is Gillian, by the way and I'm very grateful for what you have done for me. I don't intend putting on you for long…"

"You'll not leave without a proper breakfast, young lady, nor without assuring me you've somewhere decent to go to. A girl in your condition. Oh, no need to look surprised, old Mrs. Bayley can tell. Walkin' around in a storm like that, middle o' th' night an' all. What th' world is comin' to, I don't know, but enough said. I dare say as we were all young once and you're welcome to stay 'til you've sorted yourself out. I've another guest, by the way, a young man. My old pyjamas might not be the latest style, but at least you'll be decent. Your own clothes are in th' airin' cupboard." Mrs. Bayley drew in a breath, then continued. "I'll leave you to it now. I'll be in th' kitchen when you're ready to eat."

Gillian watched the old lady leave the room. She reminded her a little of Mefanway Morgan. She hoped her breakfasts were as good.

≈ ≈ ≈ ≈ ≈

"Good morning again, Mrs. Bayley," Gillian said, entering the small kitchen. "I feel more awake now. Such a beautiful morning after yesterday. Is there any more tea on the go?"

"There's always more tea on the go in this 'ouse, Gillian. Pass me your cup, there's plenty in th' pot."

Gillian handed over the cup. "Something smells delicious, Mrs. Bayley."

"Oh, yes! Bacon, eggs, sausage, black puddin's, mushrooms and fried tomato. I 'ope you're not one o' them finicky eaters that comes 'ere sometimes. Want that Continental muck they do. Not a proper breakfast that at all. You can't... I say, you can't go far on a crossunt or whatever they call them, can you? What do you say?"

"I say that I've had enough of croissants to last me a lifetime, Mrs. Bayley," Gillian laughed. But Mrs. Bayley was no longer listening. She was staring intently into the bottom of Gillian's cup.

"'ave you ever 'ad your tea leaves read before, love?"

"Well… yes." All traces of the smile disappeared from Gillian's face as she recalled that time in the kitchen at the Manor House. Mefanway's look of horror; her refusal to divulge that which she had seen. Gillian recalled the events in her life since.

"That's when all my troubles started, it seems."

Mrs. Bayley looked up from her examination of the cup, a smile on her wrinkled face. "Why so glum, lass? This is news of the best sort… and old Mrs. Bayley 'asn't been known to be wrong yet…"

Gillian peered into the bottom of the cup herself. All she could see were soggy tea leaves. "Well, what is it, Mrs. Bayley?"

"It's not an exact science, lass, but I can tell you as everything'll turn out right for you and your young man."

"Me and my young man?"

"Aye, 'appen so!" Mrs. Bayley went over to the kitchen sink and washed the cup out.

"Eeh, I can 'ear me other guest knockin' about," she said. "'e'll be wantin' 'is breakfast.. Got a motorbike, 'e 'as. A B.S.A."

Gillian looked perplexed. What had the old lady seen?

"It's a Triumph, actually, Mrs. Bayley."

Gillian turned. Her mouth dropped open.

"Rodney? How? Where?" But our heroine had no further use for words. She was in Rodney's arms, his lips pressed to hers, her hands resting on his broad shoulders as she stood on tip-toe to return his kisses. Mrs. Bayley turned away and wiped her eyes on the corner of her apron. She did so love a happy ending.

The Heiress and the Banker
Epilogue

Gillian and Rodney were married in the Autumn of 1975. A double wedding; Roxanne and Tommy being the other lucky couple.

The wedding was a top hat and tails affair arranged by the Colonel and Her Ladyship. The village church in Warmingham; the horse drawn carriages; the reception at the Manor House; everything, at their sole expense. They even sent Frank Rutter down to London in the Roller to bring Rodney's mum up to Occles-Leigh. She stayed for two weeks; a guest of the Brereton-Holbeck's.

The wedding party was a grand affair. Four families had to be considered, from very different walks of life, I might add.

However, after some initial awkwardness, all went well.

The guests included Sir William Smythe, Lady Ponsonby and, of course, Cedric, the latter bringing along his new fiancé, Lady Priscilla Moulton. Gillian noticed that the ring she wore made the one that Cedric had presented her with look like it really had been a mere bauble. Cedric told Gillian that he really did love her and always would, but as a cousin. Gillian had replied that she was relieved and the Colonel, at long last, beat Sir William at billiards. Sir William had reportedly missed a couple of easy shots, but that is by the way. It was a special occasion; the Colonel was happy; his daughter was back; he'd soon be a Grandfather and, what's more, he approved of his daughter's choice of husband. A change of heart indeed and, to help in our understanding of this, we need to back up a bit to the weekend that Rodney and Gillian were reunited at Mrs. Bayley's B&B.

On that Saturday morning, Rodney had offered… no, insisted, on escorting Gillian back to Occles-Leigh. Gillian and her TR5. Firstly, he had taken her on his motorbike to find her car. Then, with his new-found mechanical knowledge, a little bag of tools (and a little bit of luck) he got it going again. Enough for the journey home, at least. However, before going back, they had returned to Mrs. Bayley's. Rodney had wanted to stay the two nights he had intended and Gillian needed to rest up (but not enough to put her off going to the village market with Mrs. Bayley that afternoon). All in all, Gillian was glad to be back in England; glad to be with Rodney, and glad to be alive.

On the Sunday afternoon, they had returned home to Cheshire. Once in Occles-Leigh, Rodney had ridden boldly up the Manor Drive on his old Thunderbird, Gillian, in her sputtering roadster, following in his wake. This time, our hero had not put up with any of the Colonel's bullshit. Thus he had proved himself, in the eyes of the old soldier, to be a man worthy of respect and, therefore, his daughter's hand.

Yes, it had been a fine homecoming. There had been a lot of damp handkerchiefs at the Manor House that day. As for the blown inheritance? Well, what was money? The Colonel had learned his lesson; Gillian was back… and that was all that mattered.

Mrs. Bayley, quite rightly, had been a guest at the wedding and, after the reception, the newly weds went to honeymoon at her B&B. Mrs. Bayley being chauffeured home in a separate car ahead of time. The new Mrs. Watkinson was too big with child to travel far and so Stow-on-the-Moors had seemed the ideal place to start their new life together.

Rodney got his twenty pound note back from Bill at the 'White Boar', by the way. Bill had felt guilty about all the ale he had fed him and so gave it back as a souvenir; a wedding present. Rodney had had it framed, a memento of how he and Gillian first met.

The Share Shop ladies came round as well. They had known all along that that nice young man from the bank couldn't be all that bad. Otherwise, their Miss Gillian would never have had anything to do with him in the first place. That being so, Rowena, after measuring his inside leg a few more times, adjusted his suit trousers for a more comfortable fit.

Rodney and Gillian; Roxanne and Tommy; theirs weren't the only romances going on at that time. Frank Rutter had also fallen in love... with Rodney's mum. It was a fairy tale romance, although a little late in life for both of them. They were married the following spring, Frank gaining himself not only a wife and son, but *the* daughter he had always wanted.

Now, twenty or more years later, Gillian and Rodney are still together, still in love and still in Middlewich. They have two children, Delamarie, their first child, now a grown woman herself, and Bayley, blue-eyed, stalwart, the image of his father.

Roxanne and Tommy? Well, they have a passel of kids, the oldest being Andromeda. She is the image of her mother, in looks and temperament. She is also Delamarie's best friend. Together, they are a terror to the young men of Middlewich, and apart, well, they are just the same.

The tale of Delamarie Watkinson and Andromeda Boyle is, however, another story.

www.ingramcontent.com/pod-product-compliance
Lightning Source LLC
Chambersburg PA
CBHW070325130626
46556CB00007B/2732